Déjà Vu

Michal Hartstein

ISBN: 1518663109
ISBN-13: 978-1518663109

DEDICATION

This book is dedicated to my sisters: Anat and Tammi

ACKNOWLEDGMENTS

I would like to thank Mr. Yuval Gilad, Miss Michal Fridman, Mr. L.L. Fine, Mrs. Julie Phelps and Mrs. Kristie Stramaski for the great help they provided.

PART A

CHAPTER 1

At the age of sixteen and two weeks, I woke up in a hospital and couldn't remember my name.

The medical staff crowded around me, looking at me with astonishment and joy. A few minutes later, a man and a woman were ushered in to see me. The woman's eyes were filled with tears, and the man was holding her gently while they cautiously approached my bed. Personally, I was confused and scared.

They were my parents, but I didn't know them. My glazed look increased the flow of tears pouring from my mother's eyes. My father gently stroked her and leaned over to give me a kiss. I winced. I didn't know him.

"Rose," my father whispered, "I'm so glad you woke up."

Who's Rose? I thought to myself until I realized I'm Rose.

"We were so worried," my mother said, still sobbing.

I kept looking at them blankly and asked the doctor to give me a few minutes to recover.

At first, the doctor told my parents that this

confusion was natural, but a month later he had to admit that my amnesia was chronic, and my chances of remembering my past were very small. I don't know anyone who remembers the moment of his or her birth. I don't think it makes sense for a person to have memories of his life minutes after it began, but for me, in those moments, I was born again. I had no memory prior to the moments of my awakening, but my first few moments awake, after the serious accident I suffered, will forever be etched in my memory. After my frightening waking moments and the awkward meeting with my parents, I was left alone. The doctor wanted to give me time to rest, and everyone left. I found it hard to get up by myself and asked the nurse to slightly raise the back frame of my bed. Looking around, I found I was in a standard hospital room.

Because of my injuries and the fact that I was connected to quite a few monitors, I was, apparently, in a private room. I looked at the window. The sun coming through the drapes managed to blind me. I blinked and continued to survey the room. I watched the various monitors in horror. I had no idea what their purpose was, but the number of devices I was hooked up to shocked me and made me understand the seriousness of my condition. Looking toward the door of my room, I noticed another door adjacent to it. I realized immediately that this was the door to the bathroom and shower. When was the last time I peed, I wondered in horror as I lifted the blanket that covered me. I was shocked to discover myself wrapped in a large diaper. I covered myself again in embarrassment. I looked at the bathroom door again and was, again, shocked to realize that I had no idea how I actually looked. I desperately wanted to get to the bathroom, to the mirror. I rang for the nurse and she immediately appeared.

"I want to go to the bathroom."

"You can't get out of bed yet." She smiled a comforting smile at me.

"And if I need to pee?"

"When the doctor says you can stand up, we'll help you get to the bathroom. In the meantime, I'll help you while you're stuck in bed."

"Can you take this diaper off?" I asked sheepishly.

"Yes, sweetheart." She smiled that same comforting smile again.

"The truth is, what I really want is to see myself in the mirror," I smiled back, trying to emulate her smile.

"Of course." She smiled again, but this time, her smile was different. "I'll bring you a mirror."

She returned a few minutes later with a small mirror, and I looked at myself in disbelief. It's difficult to describe how strange it feels to look at yourself without recognizing the person you see, not because I'd been through a bad accident and had numerous bruises on my face, or because my hair was disheveled from lying down for such a long time. It was because I just didn't recognize my own face.

A few days later, free of the IV line and the different machines and monitors, I was moved into a room with two more hospitalized women and visited the toilet without the aid of the medical staff. After I recovered from my exertions, I made a point of brushing my hair. The swelling in my face gradually subsided, and, apart from a small scar that adorns my right cheek to this day, I went back to looking like I did before the accident.

Of course, I had no idea what I looked like before the accident. My parents brought the family photo album, but my image was foreign to me, just like those of all the other people in the album. I liked the way I looked. Perhaps if I hadn't been through the accident, I'd be like all the other teenage girls - terribly busy finding faults in my appearance - but since I had to accept my image as a fact at the age of sixteen, I liked what I saw. I was a fairly tall girl, my brown hair was long and smooth and my eyes were a changing hue of green and brown. Although I was at the peak of my adolescent years, my face was clear of the acne that many other teens had to deal with. That I was quite an attractive girl was confirmed pretty quickly by the enthusiastic stares of men and boys who visited the department. My mother said that I had a boyfriend, but I asked not to see anyone. I was very confused, and I wanted to get to know myself at my own pace.

My parents and sisters sat with me for hours, flipping through the photo albums, trying to help me regain my lost past, but I remembered none of it. Interestingly, my semantic memory wasn't damaged at all. I wouldn't have to repeat first grade. I couldn't remember who taught me to read and write or who taught me to solve equations in algebra, but I remembered how to do it.

I would learn to lie in the coming years. I would memorize every detail of the stories my family and friends would tell me, and when I wanted to make someone feel better, I'd lie and say I remembered something. In all honesty, I didn't remember a thing.

Several days later, the doctors suggested that we add some of my friends to the list of visitors. I realized that almost all of my class volunteered to visit me. I didn't know if I was popular at school. My mother claimed the kids were simply curious. My parents suggested only my two closest friends, Inbal and Daria, and my boyfriend, David, come to visit. David wanted to come first, but had to report to the recruitment office for some pre-enlistment exam, and therefore Inbal and Daria came to visit first. My sisters told me a little about Daria and Inbal, so I had no doubt which was which when they came to my room. Daria ran into my room like a hurricane and attacked me with hugs mixed with tears of joy. Inbal, who stood behind her, tugged Daria off of me and reminded her that the staff had asked them to be gentle with me.

"It's okay," I smiled. I was ready for Daria's stormy nature. "You must be Daria."

Daria was stunned as she looked at me. Despite all the preparation she'd had, it was hard for her to face the fact that she was a stranger to me. "Yes," she replied, blushing.

"How are you?" Inbal came up from behind her and gently stroked my hand.

"I'm fine," I said as I got up from my bed. "Let's go outside."

"Are you sure?" Inbal asked anxiously. "Are you able to -"

"It's okay."

We sat around a table in the courtyard of the cafeteria by the children's ward. Daria and Inbal looked sadly at a little boy with no hair, playing with his mother in the little playground.

"It's so sad." Inbal wiped tears from her eyes. "How can you deal with all this?"

I was ashamed to admit that I was so busy with myself that I hadn't yet found the time to feel sorry for the other children in the ward. "You get used to it," I said and shrugged.

"So how are you feeling?" Daria asked.

"Okay," I replied. "Nothing hurts quite so much

anymore, and the doctors say that within a week or two, I'll be back at home."

"That's great!" Inbal went back to smiling, her round face graced by huge dimples. I smiled a big smile, hoping that my smile created such beautiful dimples too. Later, in the shower adjacent to my room, I sadly discovered that it didn't, even after much effort.

"Your parents asked us to bring you all kinds of pictures and letters to refresh your memory," Daria said, raising her purse on her lap.

"I don't remember anything," I said awkwardly.

"Maybe this will help you remember?" Inbal suggested.

At this stage of my treatment, the doctors were still hoping that my memory would return. Despite their hopes, I had a feeling early on that I would never be able to remember my childhood.

Inbal and Daria spread a stack of photographs before me as well as memoirs and letters that we'd written to each other. I looked at my four-year-old self sitting between Inbal and Daria at Rebecca's Kindergarten. Our little heads were decorated with crowns made of flowers for a holiday celebration. Our friendship had begun at that kindergarten. Ever since then, and up until the accident, we'd only ever been separated for a few days at a time. We continued flipping through albums until we reached more recent ones - pictures from the scout summer camp, from school class parties. In one of the pictures I was hugging a handsome boy.

"Is this David?" I asked.

"Do you remember him?" Inbal asked hopefully.

"No... my parents told me I had a boyfriend named David."

"They didn't show you a picture of him?" Daria said

with wonder.

"They didn't have any."

"He hasn't been here yet?" Inbal was surprised.

"He was supposed to come earlier today, but had to go to the recruitment office."

"You know he was with you at the time of the accident?" Daria said.

"Yes... I was told he's the one who called the ambulance."

"He actually saw you being run over. He was standing on the other side of the road, waiting for you, when that drunk driver slammed into you. He followed the ambulance and didn't leave the emergency room for two days," Inbal said, and her eyes sparkled at the mention of his name. I had a feeling that she was in love with him herself. "Only after two days did he agree to leave."

"When I woke up, the doctors allowed only immediate family to visit me," I explained. It was a partial truth; the doctors forbade visits only for two days. After that, I was the one who refused to meet people. I was embarrassed about my memory loss and the fact that I didn't know anyone.

"So when's he coming?"

"Tomorrow," I said as I continued to carefully study the picture of the two of us.

The next day, I dozed off in my room, and when I opened my eyes, I saw a handsome young guy sitting next to my bed, looking at me with a dreamy gaze.

"How are you feeling?" he asked with a shy smile.

"Okay," I looked at him in puzzlement.

"I understand you don't remember anything." He looked at me lovingly. His blue eyes glistened with the tears he was trying to hold back.

"That's true," I said and continued to stare straight into his mesmerizing eyes.

"So you have no idea who I am..." he said in a sad voice and lowered his eyes. As he did so, a single tear trickled down his cheek.

"I'm sorry."

"I'm David."

He was much more handsome than in the picture I'd seen the day before.

"You're David, my boyfriend?"

"Yes," he said, biting his lip. He closed his eyes and took a deep breath.

"David, I'm sorry," I said and made him open his tearful eyes. "I honestly don't remember anyone... it's not personal."

"I know," he said and took my hand.

I was taken aback. I didn't know him, and my reluctance startled him.

"I love you," he said, and his words meant nothing to me. He was a fairly good-looking guy, but a complete stranger to me.

I said nothing. I didn't love him. I loved no one. I had no past. How could I love anyone? Love isn't an emotion that can be created out of thin air.

"How did it go at the recruitment center yesterday?" I tried to change the subject.

"Okay," he said in a disappointed voice. "I managed to raise my army profile." Obviously, I couldn't remember what his profile was to begin with and why he had to try and raise it. "The military doctor said I won't have any problem now, joining the paratroopers."

"Great," I smiled.

He smiled a shy smile. The last time we spoke we were lovers, and now we were like two strangers. In my eyes, this was exactly what we were.

"I brought you something," he said, and he handed me a small box.

Inside the box lay a gold ring with a small green stone. "I wanted to give you this on your birthday, but then everything happened," he said sadly. "It's pure gold with a real emerald, the one you liked most in the jewelry shop we visited a couple of weeks before the accident. I checked. It's the stone of love and health."

I found it hard to hear him say the word 'love' again, but I couldn't hurt him. I looked at him inquiringly. Although he was only a boy, not yet eighteen, his body was as solid and muscular as that of a man. I knew he was the captain of the school basketball team and tended to work out a lot. In my encounter with Inbal and Daria the day before, Inbal told me, her eyes shining with admiration, how he was doing everything he could to get into the elite paratroop squad, which was why it was urgent for him to report to the recruiting office.

"Maybe you could tell me how we met?" I asked him. Perhaps that would reunite me with my emotions.

He smiled a white-toothed grin and began to tell me how he had first noticed me when I represented the school in a debate. "I came up to you at the end of the competition and told you that you'd convinced me to become a vegetarian."

"I'm a vegetarian?" I asked in disbelief.

"Absolutely not," he laughed. "That's exactly the point - you were asked to represent that opinion. When I approached you, you looked at me with a perplexed face and made it clear that you weren't a vegetarian and honestly thought that vegetarianism wasn't a good life choice." So, my rhetorical ability made David fall deeply in love with me, and now I couldn't convince him to stop.

Now that the visiting restrictions had been lifted, he made a point of visiting me every day and rehashed more moments we'd experienced together. I discovered, to my amazement that, about two weeks before the accident, we'd celebrated our one-year anniversary as boyfriend and girlfriend, and as a result of that celebration, I'd lost my virginity. I was, to be honest, embarrassed by the discovery… I had no one I could talk to about the subject. They were all strangers to me. A few months later, I could only confirm the fact that I wasn't a virgin from a visit to the gynecologist.

David wanted us to be a couple again. He was madly in love with me and wanted us to pick up our relationship from where we'd left off, but I couldn't do it. I loved no one, but I understood that I had to learn to love my parents and my sisters again, and perhaps even my friends. However, I felt I didn't have to learn to love David again. I felt it was too much love to relearn all at once. I had no room in my heart. Gradually, he realized there was no place for him in my heart and stopped visiting me. When I returned to the high school where we both studied, he'd ask me how I was doing from time to time, and talk to me, but we didn't go back to being a couple. No girl took my place and, a year later, when I became a senior, David was recruited into the army, and I was released from the distress that his presence in the high school entailed.

My past memories were soon replaced with new memories. I learned to know and love my family, and my best friends returned to being the center of my world, as they had been before the accident. We never ran out of topics of conversation, and my accident just broadened them because Daria and Inbal enjoyed retelling our childhood memories.

Inbal was a gentle and dreamy girl. The spare time she had that wasn't spent with us or at school, was used for reading. She was the librarian's favorite student and always dreamed of becoming a heroine in a Jane Austen novel. In her dreams, Mr. Darcy would fall madly in love with her, they'd get married and have five children at the very least. Inbal was an only child, which probably explained why she dreamed of a large family. Even though her family had pretty meager means, throughout all of high school, she always had enough money for a night out. She had a waiting list of parents begging her to babysit their children in the evenings and on holidays.

Daria, in contrast, was the third of four children, and her biggest dream was to live alone. She was a beautiful girl, slender and tall. Her blue eyes sparkled because of her golden complexion and dark hair. She received much attention everywhere she went, but it wasn't enough for her, and at home, being one of four children, she felt seriously deprived of proper attention.

I soon realized that I was the glue of the trio. Daria and Inbal actually had to share me. Alone, they couldn't be friends. A large void separated their two different approaches to life. Occasionally I wondered if they could even tolerate each other. They also used to gossip to me, one about the other. That's how I learned from Inbal that Daria was shocked when David chose me over her to be his girlfriend. Daria was neither in love with David, nor took any interest in him, but when the captain of the basketball team expressed interest in me, it awoke Daria's envy. I learned from Inbal that Daria was jealous of me and David, and I learned from Daria that Inbal was, indeed, madly in love with David, but as was expected of a loyal friend, she faithfully kept her distance and said nothing about it, even after the story between David and myself ended.

Since I personally felt that there was no relationship between David and me, I didn't understand Inbal's caution: I had no problem with David being hers or anyone else's. I felt like he was never mine.

CHAPTER 2

Four years after the accident, I met my husband at Daria's army discharge party.

When Daria was released from the army, Inbal and I still had three months to serve. She, of course, marked the occasion with a huge party with dozens of guests. Those who didn't know Daria could assume, mistakenly, that she'd enjoyed every moment of her military service. Before she'd enlisted, Daria had been sure she'd be accepted into the military choir. Inbal and I were a little less convinced, but didn't ever dare express our honest opinions. In our small high school she was the undisputed star, always occupying the stage with her hypnotic and attractive performances, but she lacked exceptional singing skills. No one pointed out to her that, in our high school, she didn't have much competition, but in the military, the selection was nationwide. For two years, we had to listen to her conspiracy theories about how only people with connections were accepted into the choir, or they were accepted through nepotism. She claimed that, because she had no such ties, she had to serve on a remote base as an education coordinator.

Daria went around the club surrounded by friends and admirers. She was wearing a light-colored mini dress that showed off her tanned skin. She was drunk from all the attention. We went over to her as she talked over two tall young men - one was very thin with curly hair and a tired look on his face, and the other had a solid physique and an almost shaved head, which actually was the last stop before full baldness. His masculine facial features compensated for his premature baldness, making him look quite charming.

"Inbal! Rose!" She jumped on us. "I'm so glad you came."

"As if we could have missed this party!" I smiled warmly.

"Inbal said she wasn't sure she'd be coming." Daria looked at Inbal accusingly.

"I was supposed to stay on the base for the entire weekend," Inbal tried to defend herself.

"What's important is that all of us are here," I said, and the three of us had a group hug.

"Meet…" Daria introduced the two men who stood beside her as we approached. "Amir," she pointed to the curly guy, " and …" she tried to remember.

"Asi." The bald guy smiled at me and held out his hand.

I shook his hand, and he blushed slightly. Daria didn't miss the guy's excitement and embarrassment and rushed to focus the attention on her.

"Amir," she laid her hand lightly on Amir's shoulder, "is our new operations officer, and Asi is his friend from basic training."

"Where are you based?" Asi was still staring at me,

and I turned my gaze toward Inbal in embarrassment. "Oh, sorry, where are you both based?" Asi corrected himself.

"I'm in Zrifin and Inbal is in Tel Hashomer," I answered for the both of us.

"Nice."

Inbal realized pretty quickly that she wasn't needed there and went to talk with her other friends. Daria, for her part, once more refused to believe that a man who knew the both of us could prefer me to her. Throughout the entire evening, she fawned over Amir and Asi, who was constantly looking for my attention. He wanted us to meet up again after the party, and Daria turned his invitation into a double date.

A week later, Amir, Asi, Daria and I met up at a small café. In the quiet café, with its dim lighting, it was easier to have a conversation. Daria continued with her efforts to conquer Asi. The waitress brought the desserts, and in the background, the song "Kiss Me" by Sixpence None the Richer began to play.

"Wow," Daria rejoiced, "I just love this song." She pulled me up from the table and began to dance with me. There was no designated place for dancing, and no one else got up and danced, but it didn't stop Daria from dancing to her favorite song. I knew she really did like the song, but I also knew she was just taking advantage of the situation. The lighting and the black mini-dress she wore, combined with the fact that she could move her body sensually, created a trap that would lure any man. Only very few could withstand it. I refused to be part of Daria's one-woman-show and sat down at my place. Daria wasted no time and pulled Asi toward her. Asi began to dance awkwardly with her. The fact that he found it embarrassing didn't stop him from turning the song's lyrics into a reality by kissing her that very same night while walking her home.

Amir and I were eventually left alone.

"So you're stationed in Zrifin?" Amir tried to get me to talk.

"Yes."

"Where?"

"The 12th Training Base Camp."

"Isn't that a rookie training base?"

"Yes, it is."

"So, what are you doing there?"

"I'm a corporal."

"Interesting."

"Very."

We sat in embarrassing silence. The conversation was strained.

"You know Daria from school?"

"From kindergarten."

"Oh, wow..." He was impressed. "Well done. I was in the United States with my parents and only came back when I was in second grade, and later on we moved around, so I don't have any friends from way back."

"Wow, lucky you."

"That I moved?"

"No," I laughed, "that you got to grow up in a different country."

"I don't remember a thing," he said, and I fell quiet. Did he suffer from amnesia too?

"Why?"

"I don't know... I have fragments of memories of our stay in the United States. We were there for a total of three years, and I was very young. Do you remember yourself in kindergarten?"

"I don't remember anything that happened to me before the age of sixteen."

That surprised him. "What do you mean?"

"I had an accident when I was sixteen, and everything that happened to me before the accident was erased from my memory."

"You're not serious…" he said in a manner implying it was both a statement and a question.

"I am. Really." I looked down. My amnesia wasn't a secret, but I didn't often share my personal story with people, certainly not after such a short acquaintance.

"Wow." His eyes opened wide once again. "This is the first time I've ever met someone who's forgotten their past. You're telling me you really don't remember a thing?"

"Absolutely nothing."

"Not even your mom and dad?"

"Not even my name."

"No way!" He rubbed his face with both hands. "Then you had to learn to read and write again at sixteen?"

"No, my semantic memory wasn't damaged."

"What does that mean?"

"It means I remembered how to speak, write and read, even in foreign languages. I remembered how to solve mathematical equations and all sorts of historical facts."

"Did you remember your friends?"

"No. I told you - I didn't remember anything from my private life."

"But you still continued being their friend."

"Well, there must have been a reason we became friends before." I smiled.

"If I had to guess, I wouldn't have imagined you and

Daria being childhood friends."

"Why?"

"She's so 'out there' and you're so quiet."

"I'm not that quiet. It's just hard to stand out next to Daria."

"True enough." He laughed. "Daria is quite a character."

I didn't want to gossip about Daria with a guy I barely knew. "That's what's so fun about her; there's never a dull moment." I smiled, and Amir had to agree.

Amir and I kept in touch over the phone. The two of us had to stay two consecutive weeks in our bases, and the nice long conversations we had late into the night made our reunion thrilling and romantic. He was my first serious boyfriend after David. Amir laughed and said that the Madonna song, "Like a Virgin," was written about me. I'd lost my virginity to David, but, with Amir, I really did feel like a virgin. My relationship with Amir didn't start with stormy passion. Amir was calm and considerate, qualities that I learned to appreciate and love over the years. He was fairly handsome, but not the kind of man that made my heart miss a beat with a first glance. We didn't fall in love at first sight. We were a couple of opposites who learned to complement each other perfectly. I would create drama in my personal life and our relationship, and he, with his natural calm and composure, would always reassure me and restore peace to our lives.

Surprisingly, Daria and Asi's relationship continued as well. Maybe the fact that Asi wasn't as easy to get as some of Daria's previous admirers was the reason that he became her permanent boyfriend. Inbal was alone. For months I felt embarrassed and uncomfortable when Daria and I enjoyed romantic moments in our relationships while Inbal was still all alone, absorbed in her novels and fantasizing about her Mr. Darcy. We occasionally tried to go out, just the three of us, without boyfriends, so she wouldn't feel out of place, but almost always the conversation was filled with Amir and Asi stories, and Inbal inevitably felt left out.

Ten months after Daria and I found love, Inbal found love too. In truth, this love was always there. Inbal and I were released from our army duty and planned to go on an extended trip to the United States before starting university. One evening, while I was working as a waitress in a dimly lit pub, Inbal went to a lecture about the United States at the tourist center. There, she ran into David, my first boyfriend and the love of her youth. He was planning a trip to India, Inbal's true destination of choice, a place I would never agree to go to. Inbal had all sorts of dreams about a trip that would bring her closer to her 'spiritual self,' and I promised her that she could also be spiritual in the Nevada desert or the Rocky Mountains. David and the trip to India won, of course, and Inbal got to go on the trip of her dreams with David. Before they left, she swore to me that he was just a good friend from high school, but when they returned, she sat me down for a talk.

"Rose," she said hesitantly, "you know you're like a sister to me."

"Of course."

"And I really think that things like this shouldn't happen, but I think our circumstances are different."

"What are you talking about?" I began to worry a little.

"David..."

"What about him?" I faked innocence; I had a feeling

that this had started before they'd even left the country.

"In India..." she looked down sheepishly, "you know... I mean, you don't... I can't explain it. India has a very special atmosphere."

"You and David are together?" I cut her suffering short.

She looked at me with a surprised look. "How did you know?"

"I figured..." I shrugged.

"You don't mind?" Inbal, like many others, refused to believe that my memory had been completely erased.

"Inbali, how many times do I have to tell you I don't feel like I ever was David's girlfriend?"

"But still -"

"There is no 'but still.' Even if I did remember anything, many years have passed since then. David isn't my property."

"I feel bad..." She started to cry and I reached over and hugged her.

"You don't have to feel bad about it. If you're in love, then you should celebrate your love! I shouldn't play any part in this story."

She gave me a sheepish smile. "You're incredible."

"You're more." I kissed her. "Besides, I have a little secret to tell you."

"What?" she asked curiously.

"Amir and I are planning on getting married," I said, revealing the engagement ring Amir had given me two weeks earlier.

"Wow!" she said enthusiastically. "How beautiful!"

"Believe me - David isn't even a distant memory for me."

Inbal laughed. "When are you getting married?"

"I don't know... probably not in the next two years."

"So why propose now?"

"It's kind of a declaration. Both of us are starting out studies in less than a month, so we're not in a hurry."

The relationship between Inbal and David didn't bother me at all. If anything, I was actually more comfortable in Inbal's company because she was no longer alone. David was also uncomfortable around me at first, but over time, he realized that I had no reservations about his and Inbal's love.

CHAPTER 3

Daria and Asi got married first.

To be precise, Daria and Asi decided to get married right after Daria found out that Amir had proposed to me, which was just over a year after Amir and I became a couple. I was surprised by his proposal. At this stage of our lives, we were already living together and knew it was a serious relationship, but Amir wasn't a great romantic; the fact that he bothered to buy me a real, though small, diamond ring and get down on one knee at the same café where we'd first gone with Daria and Asi amazed me.

Of course, I said, "Yes," although it was clear to both of us that we wouldn't be getting married anytime soon. We both began our studies: I was studying economics and accounting and he was majoring in software engineering. I made my living mostly from temporary waitressing jobs, and he spent more than half his nights guarding empty buildings for a living. We didn't have the time or the money to get married, but it was important to Amir to 'show seriousness,' as he explained to me later.

About six months after Amir gave me the 'commitment' ring, as we liked to call it, we met up with Asi and Daria.

"What's this?" Daria pulled my hand toward her and looked closely at the diamond ring that adorned my finger. "Is this new?"

"Not really -"

"It's the first time I've seen this ring."

"It means we don't get to see each other enough. Or you don't look at me enough," I smiled.

"Believe me, I look at you a lot." I didn't doubt it; Daria always made sure to scan all the people around her, more specifically all the girls, from head to toe, making sure that no one met her standards. "The fact that we hardly see each other is another story altogether... you know how busy I've been with school and work." Daria rolled her eyes. She already had her beauty diploma and had a job. She didn't have to deal with the burden of academic studies in addition to waitressing.

"Well?" She wouldn't let it go and went on whining, "What is this ring?" She fingered the ring. "Is it a diamond?" she asked, surprised.

"A small one," I apologized.

"It looks quite like an engagement ring."

"Why only 'like' one?" Amir burst into the conversation.

Daria's blue eyes widened in amazement. "Are you getting married?"

"Yes," Amir said.

"At some point," I added.

"You can't be serious!" she almost shouted. "This is how you tell me?"

"There's still nothing to tell. We don't even have a date yet. We just decided to declare our intentions."

"Declare?" she said in a defeated tone. "If I hadn't asked, you wouldn't have even told me."

"Because there still isn't much to tell."

Daria wasn't reassured. The friendly gathering ended early with a bad atmosphere. I wasn't sure if it was because I didn't tell her, or that she was hurt that she wasn't the first to receive a marriage proposal, but a few days later Asi dropped down on one knee, and almost a year later, Asi and Daria were married in a lavish ceremony.

At Asi and Daria's wedding, Amir asked me when I wanted to get married. He was afraid that I was jealous or nervous. I wasn't jealous. Nor was I nervous. I knew he wanted me and that someday we'd get married. A year later, we were also standing at the altar and a few months after that, Inbal and David exchanged rings as well.

In less than two years, the three of us had gotten married and each wedding was different from the others. Our wedding was pretty standard: dusty hall, cliché flower arrangements and an ambitious three-course meal that tasted dull and was served by exhausted waiters. Daria and Asi's wedding was all luxury and innovation. Asi's father was a successful importer who made sure his beloved son's wedding lacked nothing. Daria switched between three dresses during the evening, which revolved all around her. The wedding was held over a pool against the backdrop of impressive water fountains, and the dinner was gourmet fare. Since I got married after Daria, it was impossible to say that I even tried to copy her wedding. While I enjoyed her wedding, which was fancy and joyful, I didn't have the time or the money to invest too much in planning my wedding because I was a student and a full time waitress. I didn't try on dozens of dresses. I didn't sit for hours planning the design of the tables. Nor did I attend countless other weddings just to see the various bands available, so that I could design the perfect event for myself. Amir and I were exhausted from school and work. This was certainly reflected in our wedding, which was dull and drained, just like us.

Of the three weddings, the wedding that was most beautiful and exciting, in my opinion, was actually Inbal and David's. They spent perhaps half of what Amir and I spent and most probably a fifth of the cost of Daria and Asi's wedding. It was a modest and touching event. Inbal and David invited a handful of friends and close family to a small and intimate café on the beach at Herzliya. The food served at the wedding was simple, but tasty, and the makeshift dance floor was full of friends who danced and rejoiced until the small hours. Inbal and David promised to be faithful to each other at sunset. Inbal's eyes sparkled when David put her wedding ring on her finger. She looked at him with such love that my heart twisted in jealousy. I loved Amir, but never did we exchange glances with such love as Inbal and David had.

Inbal had made her dream come true. She married her childhood sweetheart, who learned to love her as she loved him. Throughout the evening, Inbal and David didn't leave each other even for a moment. It was the most modest and happy wedding I've ever attended. Of the three of us, Inbal had always been the least attractive one, and though I was happy that she and David had a loving relationship, they always looked like an unbalanced pair because of the difference in their appearances. He was one of the most remarkable men

I've ever seen – tall and muscular with masculine facial features and dreamy blue eyes. He could have had any girl he wanted, and out of all the girls in the world, he chose Inbal, who had always been a little chubby with brown-blonde curly hair that she always found difficult to manage. Her features were nice, but because she always was slightly overweight, her face was too plump to be considered beautiful. The only thing she shared with David in terms of appearance was an amazing pair of eyes. David had dreamy blue eyes and she had huge gray-green eyes. In her simple wedding dress, with makeup that emphasized her eyes and her braided hair, she was amazingly beautiful. All her delicate inner beauty, which David had learned to know and admire, broke out in full force on her wedding day, and David couldn't take his eyes off her.

This was the first time I remembered being jealous of Inbal, and I hated every minute. Inbal had always been a loyal and loving friend. She always knew how to offer praise and give to others. For the first time since the accident, I felt that maybe I'd made a mistake by rejecting David. All that joy and love could have been mine. Mine.

And I'd given it up.

Since I had no recollection of my childhood, I didn't remember emotions either. I didn't remember ever experiencing jealousy. Since the accident, I'd had no reason or time to be envious. It's not that I wasn't jealous of anyone. I envied a student who got a better grade than me in a test, or a soldier in the army who received a certificate of merit at my expense. The Dean's List that was hanging on the faculty notice board made my jealousy stir as well. I was on the list, but not in first place. It's not that I'd never envied, but never before did jealousy eat me up from the inside as it did after Inbal and David's wedding. Maybe it was because I've always sensed that the jealousy I felt was repairable - I could learn better for the next test, or be a more disciplined soldier. But this great love that Inbal enjoyed could have been mine, and I'd lost it forever.

Amir was a great spouse, handsome, hardworking and educated. He cared for me and loved me. I had no real reason to be jealous. But the jealousy that was born the day of Inbal and David's wedding became a part of me. For years, I'd secretly sniggered at Daria, with her conduct always fueled by envy and her desire to present herself as more perfect than others. Unlike me, Daria's jealousy was motivated by materialism. She always had to show everyone that she had the best out there before anyone else had it. Daria, for example, didn't really appreciate Inbal's wedding. It was far too simple for her taste, not her style at all. She wasn't envious in the least.

As far as Daria was concerned, she'd won because she finally had the most beautiful party. As a child, Daria's birthday parties were the most simple and meager of all. Her parents were simple, warm-hearted people, and they did everything they could to make their four children happy, but they didn't have the means to indulge them. When we were in third grade, Daria's mother organized a birthday party for her, inviting the entire class, just a week after Oren's birthday. Oren was the richest kid in class. The gap between the two parties was so big that Daria could barely raise a smile at her own birthday party. Just a week after the whole class had enjoyed an abundance of sweets, a magician who amazed the kids with his talents, and prestigious party prizes, the same children gathered in Daria's simple living room and enjoyed a handful of snacks and sweets, mostly made by her mother. Daria's big sister organized the party games and gave out prizes that were very simple. When Oren won one of the games, he received a balloon as a reward. "Balloon?" he sniggered when he received his prize from Daria. "This isn't a prize!" he declared and then resumed his seat, tossing the balloon to Sigal, who agreed to accept the pitiful award. That was the last time Daria hosted the class at her home. She even played down her Bat Mitzvah celebration and said she was celebrating only with her family. Thanks to Asi, she had finally organized an event she could be proud of. Daria's wedding was certainly one of the most impressive and exclusive weddings I'd been invited to, but for me, Inbal and David's wedding was all I could have ever wanted, and stupidly gave up on.

Two weeks after the wedding, Inbal sent out wedding pictures by e-mail. For two weeks, I'd tried to convince myself that it was all in my head and I was imagining my feelings, but the images only fanned my jealousy. Inbal and David looked even more in love in the pictures than I remembered.

"What is it?" Amir asked when he saw me studying the computer screen with such great care.

"Pictures from Inbal and David's wedding."

"Really?" Amir pulled up a chair and sat next to me. "Let me see."

Amir ran through the images and roared with laughter when he came to a picture of him and Asi making faces behind Daria's back.

"What do you think about the pictures?"

"Pretty pictures."

"And the wedding?"

"Nice wedding."

"You're not sorry we didn't have a wedding like that?"

"What do you mean, a wedding like that?"

"A more modest style."

"Your parents would never, ever put on such a small wedding." He was right.

"But you don't think this wedding was more exciting than ours?"

"No," he frowned. "Why? Do you think it was more exciting?"

"I don't know... " But, really, I did know. "Look at this picture." I focused on a picture of Inbal and David looking into each other's eyes. "Look how excited they are, how in love they are."

"Obviously they were excited, but they don't seem to be more excited or in love than any other of the dozens of couples I know."

"Including us?" I asked uncertainly.

"Especially us," he laughed and I joined him.

He was able to reassure me, but not for long. The jealousy in me grew, and instead of chucking it out, I tended it with dedication and obsession, and it became an integral part of me. The more I dug deeper in me, the more the jealousy intensified. I was disgusted with myself every time I tried to showcase our relationship as better than theirs. Even Amir felt it, and he wasn't usually quick to pick up on emotions. Whenever we met up with Inbal and David, I tried to find a crack in the wall of love that surrounded them. I wanted to discover that not everything was perfect. I tried to forcibly drag them into arguments and put them in uncomfortable situations.

One of these occasions occurred about three and a half months after Inbal and David had gotten married. We met with them and Daria and Asi to see a movie, and Inbal excitedly told us how, a few days earlier, David had surprised her and invited her out to the café where they were married in honor of their first hundred days as a married couple. Amir and I hadn't celebrated our first hundred days as a married couple, and when I counted the days in my head, I discovered - to my dismay - that Amir and I had no excuse for forgetting that exciting, momentous date. We were both on summer break from university, and my residency with my large accounting firm had not yet begun.

"We celebrate each and every day!" I said and flashily leaned against Amir, who embraced me warmly. For Amir, the embrace was enough, but I continued to fawn over him and make out with him throughout the evening. He didn't stop me, but I felt he was embarrassed.

"What's going on with you tonight?" Daria asked me as we sat drinking coffee after the movie ended.

"What do you mean?" I asked innocently.

"I don't know," she shrugged. "You're all over Amir, acting as if you only met a couple of days ago."

"I'm just horny," I whispered in her ear and giggled. "I'm probably ovulating." She rolled her eyes and turned her focus to the group discussion. Daria had noticed my odd behavior, but she didn't understand it. It just drove me even crazier. Daria, who was always busy making comparisons and presenting herself as the best of our trio, wasn't bothered by Inbal and David and their expressions of affection and romance. She was happy with what she had because she felt she was the most beautiful and rich one in the group. I wanted to be happy with what I had too.

But I couldn't.

On the way home, Amir asked me about all my

relentless touching and caressing throughout the evening.

"I just felt like it."

"I thought you didn't like excessive demonstrations of emotion in public."

"Why would you think that?"

"I remember when we met with my cousin and his girlfriend, you were shocked by the way they were all over each other."

"Because it was over exaggerated."

"You exaggerated tonight too."

"I did not -"

"You surely did," he said loudly. "I understand you want to show Inbal that she's not the only one in love, but that was just ridiculous."

His accurate assessment was too painful. I bit my lip and didn't respond. There was no point. I was offended, even though I deserved it.

When we got home, after a long and quiet ride, he said softly, "You have to understand that nobody has a perfect life, no one's perfect. No one has a perfect husband or a perfect job and I've heard that there's no such thing as perfect children either."

At that moment, he was just perfect for me.

CHAPTER 4

A little more than two years after Inbal and David celebrated their hundred day anniversary, I was on my way to Jerusalem for my graduation ceremony, where I would be receiving my accounting degree. I felt unwell and didn't want to go to Jerusalem and back just to get my diploma, but I knew that my parents would never forgive me if didn't allow them to watch me officially become a Certified Public Accountant.

The ride up to Jerusalem only made me feel worse, and the second time we had to stop for me to throw up, my mother asked me discreetly if I was pregnant. The thought of being pregnant never crossed my mind until that moment. I was twenty-seven, but I'd only just finished my internship. I wanted to build a career before I became a slave to children. We stopped at the drugstore and Mom ran in and bought a pregnancy test kit.

"Aren't you supposed to try these tests in the morning?"

"If you're throwing up, it's probably not the

beginning of the pregnancy. We may be able to see an answer already," she said knowingly.

Five minutes later I returned to the car with a can of Coke to calm my nausea and the knowledge that I was going to become a mother. I lied to my mother and told her that the answer was negative. I thought that Amir should be the first to know. The long and dreary ceremony refused to end. Even reuniting with some former school friends couldn't make me forget this surprising turning point in my life, which wasn't in any way related to financial reports or tax laws.

I forced my smiles, so distracted that I almost missed my moment on stage. Thoughts kept running around in my head. At first, I couldn't understand how it had happened. I took my pills regularly. Could I have missed one? It was the annual report season... Maybe I hadn't noticed. After I realized that I wasn't the second woman in history to get pregnant by the Holy Spirit, I started on the self-pity. I'd just finished my internship, and all the other interns had already begun looking for prestigious jobs as accountants and financial officers, and I knew that, no matter how talented I was, very few companies would want to hire a young mother for a senior position. The thought of getting an abortion crossed my mind, and it startled me. Because of the accident and the fact that I'd gotten my life back, I attributed great respect to the value of life. I was terrified that it could even occur to me to end the life of a living creature that was growing inside of me.

During the pregnancy, I hated and loved my little embryo. I liked to feel the new life inside me, but I hated the thought that the life I had planned for myself was about to be destroyed. Around me, more and more interns found work that was, more or less, prestigious -

even those who began their internships after me, even those I thought weren't as professional as I was. I wasn't job hunting. I saw no point. The feelings of jealousy and missed opportunities that accompanied me after Inbal's wedding came back to haunt me. Again, I felt I had no control over my jealousy because I couldn't fix it. I was pregnant and nothing could change that fact.

The only little bonus of my pregnancy was that, for the first time, I felt Inbal was jealous of me. I hated the pleasant sensation her jealousy gave me, but I couldn't ignore it. Inbal had dreamed of being a mother ever since she could remember. I also had no doubt that she'd be a great mom. I didn't know anyone more sensitive and patient than she was. Unlike me, Inbal didn't even attempt to conceal or obscure her envy. She was jealous and she just said it aloud. I was so sorry I didn't have the ability to be as honest and open as she was. I felt that, although the dream of becoming a mother was at the center of her being, and even though she had to watch in despair as her friends around her began to swell, the fact that she didn't hide her emotions helped her cope with her emotions. While Inbal was trying to get pregnant long before my news came out, Daria realized she was out of the race only when she found out I was expecting. Daria was the least maternal character I knew; she was the one who always needed to be taken care of. Were it not for my pregnancy, I don't believe she would have even thought about having a family. But as expected, a month after Amir and I announced our pregnancy, Daria and Asi also announced their own impending happy event.

Nofar, my eldest daughter, was born after two nightmarish days of contractions. It was a fitting end to a pregnancy that managed to exhaust me physically and, especially, mentally. I felt as though the guilt that had accompanied me throughout the entire pregnancy, because of my unwillingness to become a mother, poured through my umbilical cord and fed my little girl with anger and hatred toward me. During the ongoing birth, I had a terrible feeling that she didn't want to come out. When they put her on my stomach, I looked at her blankly. I felt nothing. Amir softly stroked my forehead and said excitedly that she was simply stunning. I didn't think she was stunning. I thought she was small and crumpled. The difficult birth had taken its toll on her too.

"You can hug and kiss her," the midwife encouraged me.

I felt terrible that I had to be given instructions on how to love my daughter. I didn't want to hug and kiss anyone. I just wanted to sleep. I was exhausted.

The nurse threw me a surprised look while Amir smiled and leaned down to kiss his daughter. Eventually, I hugged and kissed her, and then the nurse took her for some initial treatment. I was glad. I didn't know what I was supposed to do or feel, and what I wanted more than anything was to rest. The baby weighed only seven pounds, but as soon as the nurse picked her up, I felt as if a heavy load was lifted off me.

Amir thought I was suffering from postpartum depression. I didn't think he was right. Although I wasn't happy, I knew in advance I wouldn't be happy. I didn't want to be a mother at this stage of my life. This reality was forced on me, and it took me a while to get used to it. Over time, I learned to get used to little Nofar, but she didn't get used to me, which only worsened my feelings of guilt that accompanied me from the moment I found out I was carrying her in my womb. I loved watching her as she slept. She looked so calm and sweet. She probably dreamed of another mother. Apart from a small birthmark on her right shoulder, she was a perfect, beautiful baby. She had a thin veil of hair, huge eyes and rosy, plump cheeks. When sleeping, her tiny hands clenched into tiny fists, ready to fight her mother. In those moments, when she slept, dreaming of another mother, I lay down and stroked her tenderly as I dreamed I was a different mother… a calm and patient mother.

Although I tried to feed her, she simply refused to accept the milk my body produced for her. I gave her my erect nipple, she sucked it for a few seconds and then pulled away in distaste, as if I was giving her poison and not milk. She felt my hidden rejection of her and rejected me back. She would cry for days and calm down only when Amir came home and picked her up in a loving and protective embrace.

"This baby just can't stand me," I said to Amir with a tired look as he cradled her in his arms and looked at her lovingly. "She never calms down with me like she does with you."

"You're just imagining it. You're with her the entire day, and she's just tired now. On weekends, when I'm with her, she cries with me too."

"Not like she cries with me," I sighed, but he just wouldn't listen.

A new media trend was doing the rounds: mothers describing how parenting was not what they'd anticipated, how no one told them that being a mother entailed getting up three times a night and being subjugated to a small and demanding creature, even when you're wiped out. Amir showed me these stories every time a celebrity released her thoughts, acting as if she was the first mother ever to confess that being a mother isn't all it was cracked up to be. He thought that I, too, was just surprised by parenthood, but that wasn't the case. On the contrary, I was very conscious of the sacrifices it forced me to make. I was sitting at home, bored out of my mind, with a child who felt that her mother didn't want her. Occasionally, they called me from work to ask me something and so I kept up to speed with all the colleagues who'd progressed and left for management positions. I felt left behind. I was once on the Dean's List… I could've chosen almost any role that was offered to my coworkers, but, instead, I sat at home and changed diapers for a restless baby.

I minimized my meetings with Daria and Inbal at that time. The fact that Inbal was jealous of my baby didn't make me as happy as it did during the pregnancy. I envied her even more now, because she was free as a bird. Daria's pregnancy was very photogenic. I didn't see it with my own eyes, but Daria made sure to update us with pictures of her growing stomach with repugnant insensitivity given the difficulties Inbal was going through. Daria and Asi's baby, Roy, was born a month before I returned to work. Daria was hoping that I'd extend my maternity leave so that we could spend mom time together, but I was impatient to return to work, mainly to get some time off the overwhelming routine of motherhood.

Upon my return to work, everyone wanted to see pictures of little Nofar. My out-of-the-ordinary motherhood hit me again; I hardly had any pictures of her. I didn't feel the need to cherish every moment of her life like other mothers who often filmed their offspring. They looked on, astonished at the meager handful of photos I managed to find on my cell phone.

"This is it?" they asked me more than once in surprise.

"I have more on the camera at home," I lied. A few days later, I snapped Nofar in a variety of flattering and cute poses and I framed the cutest picture of them all and put it on my desk. I didn't want to seem abnormal. But this photo, to me, was just photographic proof of my failure as a mother. This was actually an image that Amir took, because when I photographed Nofar, she wouldn't smile as she did with Amir. Every time I looked at the picture, I felt more and more certain of my decision: If I was a failure as a mother, at least I would become a successful career woman. If I didn't know how to give my child the love and care she needed, she would get it with all the money I earned.

On Independence Day of that year, we met up at Daria and Asi's place to watch the fireworks show from their terrace. Asi, who'd joined his father's clothing import business a few years earlier, had doubled and even tripled the business' profits, which allowed them to move to a spectacular penthouse in northern Tel Aviv. Daria was ecstatic. She'd quickly regained her original pre-pregnancy figure and boasted of the standard of living she had, which we could only dream of at this stage of our lives. Nofar crawled around Roy, who sat on the bouncer watching my toddler eyeing all of the toys scattered around him.

"Sorry about the mess," Daria apologized, and I looked around and tried to figure out what mess she was referring to. Apart from a small number of toys, her house was spotless and tidy. I couldn't remember our apartment being this neat since Nofar was born.

"You're kidding me!" I said in disbelief. She looked at

me as if she didn't understand what I meant. "What mess are you talking about?"

"This…" She pointed at a few toys scattered in the living room. Nofar had just picked up a spongy ball and put it in her mouth. Daria grimaced.

"She's putting everything in her mouth at the moment," I apologized and pulled the ball out of her mouth. She burst into tears and only stopped wailing when Amir took her up in his arms.

"Roy's still very small," she explained. "I don't know if it's okay for him to come into contact with other children's saliva."

"He'll have to get used to it at some point," I smiled. "Soon he'll be going to kindergarten."

"Why soon?" Daria wondered. "Nofar's going to kindergarten?"

"Not exactly kindergarten. It's a children's daycare, but there are four other children there. In September, she'll start kindergarten, though."

"Roy won't go to daycare until he's two."

"You're going to stay home with him?" I asked. If I was climbing the walls, I couldn't imagine how Daria would deal with watching her baby for two years.

"Of course not," she laughed. "He's with his nanny."

"He has a nanny already?" I tried to understand why Daria used the present tense.

"Of course. We've had a nanny since he was a month old."

"Really? Why?"

"I don't need to tell you what raising a baby's like," she winked. "I also hired someone who gives me childcare advice and helps me with the laundry and cooking."

"You cook?" Daria couldn't make an omelet.

"No. But I think it's important to have a cooked meal, especially when there's a baby at home."

"He eats food already?"

"Step by step."

Now the exemplary order and cleanliness were clear. Daria, who hadn't yet returned to work at her cosmetics company, had a fleet of employees: a nanny who also washed and cooked, a cleaning lady, a young beautician who took care of her company while she was on maternity leave, and even a teenager who would walk her poodle every day at noon.

Inbal and David arrived slightly late because David had to finish his shift at the fire station where he worked. As soon as Inbal came in, I knew she was pregnant. She was radiant. Inbal was never a skinny girl, so it still wasn't possible to discern any bulge in her stomach, but her whole being exuded the happiness that enveloped her. She walked into the new apartment, admired the designer features and impressive views, hugged and kissed us all, and finally leaned over and hugged Roy and Nofar warmly. On previous occasions when she'd met Nofar, she'd always picked her up and played with her, but hadn't tried to hide her jealousy and the sorrow in her eyes. Today, her gaze was full of tenderness and joy.

The fireworks began and we looked up at the crackling sky. Amir was holding Nofar, who pointed at in amazement at the colorful flashes of light. Roy began to cry hysterically, and Daria took him inside. I looked at David and Inbal. They stood and watched the sky intently. David's muscular arm was resting on Inbal's shoulder. They looked so calm and relaxed. My old jealousy returned and overwhelmed me. David was a man's man, a charming firefighter who protected his loving wife with his body. I looked back at Amir. He was a tall, handsome man, but his stomach had begun to expand and his hair was thinning. As a computer engineer in a software company, he didn't move his body as much as David did, and as the years passed, he looked older than David. Amir wasn't a romantic and protective man like David, and I loved him because of his practical nature, but, like many women, in my heart I longed for a charming man who would sweep me up in ecstasy. A few minutes later, the fireworks ended and we settled down around the dinner table on the terrace to eat the steaks Asi had cooked.

"Excellent," Inbal said with pleasure.

"Thank you," Asi smiled. Daria didn't compliment him often. She didn't touch the steak he'd prepared for her. Until she lost the extra couple of pounds from her pregnancy, she had no intention of risking any additional weight gain.

"Enjoy," Daria smiled at Inbal with a starving look.

"I am enjoying myself!" Inbal said through a mouthful of steak, with a secretive, self-assured look.

"You're looking good," Daria looked at Inbal carefully and suddenly noticed the halo surrounding her.

"Thank you," she smiled and poured herself a glass of juice.

"Did you do something with your hair?" Daria frowned. "Are you wearing makeup? There's something different about you."

"Nope," she shrugged.

Asi returned from the kitchen with a bottle of wine and started to pour everyone a glass. When he reached Inbal, she signaled with her hand that she didn't want any, and she raised her glass of juice. "I'll settle for juice for now," she said.

"You're pregnant?" Daria blurted out tactlessly.

Inbal took a deep breath, took a sip from her glass of juice and put it back on the table. We all looked at her, and she whispered with a delighted smile, "Yes!"

"Wow! Inbali!" Daria jumped up and hugged Inbal. "That's great. Get up so we can see you better." I was surprised to see Daria demonstrate such happiness. I watched her closely and discovered, to my amazement, that she was genuinely happy for Inbal. Daria was genuinely happy for her, or maybe happy to finally have a friend to share motherhood with, since I hadn't really cooperated with her.

Inbal stood up and patted her stomach. "I'm not showing yet," she apologized. "Early days…"

"What week?" I inquired.

"Tenth," she smiled at me. I put down the wine glass I was holding and went to her. We hugged in a long and affectionate embrace. Despite my envy, I was still really glad for her. She'd waited a long time for this.

"I'm so happy for you," I said quietly as we pulled apart from one another.

"I know," she whispered back, and my heart ached. She had such faith in me. It didn't even occur to her that I envied her.

We clinked five glasses of wine and a glass of juice in honor of Israel's sixty years of independence and Inbal's auspicious pregnancy. She tried to calm our joy, saying she'd already had three miscarriages, but this time all indications showed that the pregnancy was going to end with a baby.

I had trouble sleeping that night. Nofar, for once, fell asleep easily and slept soundly. Amir was snoring lightly next to me, but my thoughts wouldn't let me sleep. I felt stuck. I'd always felt like the strongest of our trio. I was the best student. I wasn't drop dead gorgeous like Daria, but I was very pretty and, in addition, I had a fascinating life story because of the accident and the amnesia. Inbal and Daria also had their own strengths, but, all in all, my advantages were stronger. I'd always gone around with the feeling that I'd achieve much in life, but suddenly I felt left behind. Daria was beautiful and rich and Inbal was in love and radiant from her pregnancy, while I was a desperate mother with a sinking career.

I wanted to be the strong one in our trio again, and after hours of thought and reflection, I realized that the way to restore my confidence and joy in life was to succeed where I thought I had the edge. I was determined to further my career. I believed that if I succeeded as an accountant, my frustrating envy of my friends would fade away. Every time I felt that jealousy burning inside of me, I was disgusted with myself. Jealousy was pushing me away from my friends, to the extent that I refrained from meeting and talking to them, because I didn't want to feel it. I didn't want the others to recognize it. The only one who knew about it was Amir, who also tried to minimize its effect in my life. I hoped that if I succeeded professionally, if others had reason to envy me, I could destroy my tormenting jealousy.

CHAPTER 5

After Independence Day and Inbal's announcement, I started an intensive search for a new job. I went to numerous interviews and screening tests, and in some cases I reached an advanced stage of the interview process, but I never got an offer. I blamed the fact that I was a mother on my failure to achieve a managerial position. It wasn't just a feeling; it was an understanding of reality. Interviewers weren't allowed to ask me questions about my parenting or my thoughts on expanding my family, but in every interview, as we reviewed my résumé together, I felt that nod; it simultaneously expressed their understanding of my delicate situation as a mother, and yet disqualified me.

After months of searching, I realized that I should lower my expectations of the coveted job, or just continue working where I was, but the work seemed boring and unrewarding. I soon realized that the even the less glamorous jobs on the market were not just sitting waiting for me. Despair began to gnaw at me. Every day I returned home in the early afternoon to my failing attempts to be a 'normal' mother. I tried to play with Nofar, but babyish games bored me, and her sharp instincts told her that I had no real desire to play and stay with her.

To pass the hours until Amir arrived home, I started going down to the park near our apartment. My encounters with other mothers of toddlers only made my utter failure as a mother clearer. Every day, I found myself trying to imitate other mothers. Over time, I learned to look less and less abnormal. I learned to sing and smile falsely at Nofar while pushing her on the swing. I learned that as long as she wasn't yet walking, I needed to bring a small blanket for her and spread it on the grass with some toys. I often looked around at the other women. They seemed to genuinely love and enjoy playing with their children; their sincere smiles and hugs were full of love and warmth. It was clear to me that not all of it was real, and that everyone wears a mask away from home, but others' efforts seemed more natural to me. Other mothers sat together, talking, sharing diaper stories and recipes for toddlers, but I found it hard to fit in. I couldn't fake interest in the conversation on topics that bored me terribly. I wondered at times whether there were more mothers like me. Although I felt abnormal, I imagined I wasn't the only mother in the world who found a conversation about breast milk supplements extremely uninteresting. Despite all my attempts to blend in with the other mothers, occasionally my real lack of interest revealed itself in public. One torrid afternoon, I sat on the grass with Nofar near several other mothers I knew from kindergarten. If it hadn't been so hot, I'd probably have chosen to sit somewhere else, but there was no other shady spot. I spread out my usual blanket and took out the usual toys.

One of the mothers admired Nofar's new dress that my mother had bought for her. I smiled with satisfaction. After a few minutes, I took out a bag of Bamba and gave Nofar one to nibble on happily.

"How old is she?" one mother asked with a worried look when she saw Nofar holding the yellow snack.

"A little more than ten months." I smiled. The other mothers wouldn't usually talk to me so I was glad for the opportunity.

"And you're already giving her Bamba?" another mother asked in surprise.

"Why not?" I was surprised at the question. "It's very soft and she's just sucking it."

"It's a peanut snack!" the first mother almost shouted. "You can't give that to her before she turns one."

"She's nearly a year old." I tried to calm things down. To be honest, I had no idea you weren't supposed to give children under a year peanuts.

"They didn't tell you this at the children's clinic?"

"No," I said and smiled. I was ashamed to admit that I'd never been to the children's clinic. Amir always took her to get the necessary shots, but I decided to pass on the developmental tests. The child seemed well developed and the pediatrician who'd seen her several times didn't think she had any problems.

"Either way, it's written in quite a few articles and books." A third mother jumped in, trying to shame me and my ignorance. "Peanuts are allergenic… you mustn't expose babies to allergenic foods. It could end in disaster."

"I don't think she's allergic to peanuts." I continued to smile, but I was burning with anger. I was angry at the audacity of these women who barely know me, yet felt comfortable enough to judge me. Mostly, though, I was angry with myself for not caring enough to read up on toddler foods.

I often wondered if I was looking for a demanding administrative job in order to realize myself, or rather to find an excuse not to have to take care of my daughter every day.

Across the globe, rumors began to circulate about a deepening economic crisis. Articles about banks closing and firms collapsing were published daily. The crisis began to seep slowly into the Israeli economy and the supply of jobs just dwindled, and with it my dream of a management career withered. The firm I worked for decided to avoid layoffs, despite the severe crisis, and chose to cut all employee wages. I now worked in the same dull, hateful job for lower wages.

In December of that year, I realized that most of the interns who'd started working at the same time I had were now in various senior positions in accounting and management. Even interns who had received their license a year or more after me had begun to find their place in the field. I had been left behind. Amir couldn't understand my unrest. I had a steady job; I had job security and wages that were slightly higher than the average. Although I'd said more than once that a managerial position would be more interesting, I didn't know that for sure. I'd never worked in a management position. Amir didn't understand the pressure on interns to move up the ranks. He wasn't sure why there should be such pressure. I'd worked for my accounting firm for a total of four years, four months of which I'd been on maternity leave. "Aren't there people in your office who've been there many more years?" he asked me more than once. There were veteran employees in the office, but in my eyes they seemed dull and uninspired. I wanted to thrive.

Amir had worked for years as a software engineer. His job description and his rank in the company never interested him. He thought that, as long as I enjoyed the work and was getting paid better than before, the job description shouldn't matter at all. He, of course, didn't understand the meaning of job descriptions in my field of work.

At Hanukkah, Inbal and David's baby girl was born. Inbal was radiant while I'd never felt more drained. I knew that in order to return to my old self, I'd have to find another job. I couldn't stand that searing jealousy that ate at me every time a friend from school or work got promoted. I hated myself for gloating every time I heard about a company closing and someone I knew got fired. Inbal's happiness blinded me completely. I couldn't look at her and her idyllic family. I had to prove to everyone that I could fulfill my dreams.

While preparing the annual reports for one of my clients, I learned that the company was looking for a new chief bookkeeper. The title startled me. I was a Certified Public Accountant (CPA), not a bookkeeper. The fact that they added 'chief' to the title didn't make it any more attractive to me. The woman who was leaving was a bookkeeper by profession, although with the highest qualification in the field, but not a CPA like me. My reluctance to try for it disappeared when I realized that the job offered a salary that was higher by almost fifty percent than my current salary in the accounts office.

Two years after I became a CPA, I'd finally found a new job. Smart Green, which engaged in the development and production of ecological goods for industry, was a stable company, and the work was very interesting. Shoshana, the chief bookkeeper I was replacing, was retiring, but sat with me for a month and patiently shared the secrets of the role. The accounts department included two other employees: the bookkeeper who worked with the customers and the bookkeeper who worked with the suppliers. My job was to supervise them, to work with the banks, make adjustments and prepare salaries.

I'd found a job that was fun and challenging, and my salary jumped significantly. I should have been happy, but I was ashamed to tell people that I was employed as a bookkeeper (a chief, mind you) and not as an accountant. When friends or family members took an interest in my new job, I told them I was employed as head of the accounts department, and sometimes I just lied and said I was the accountant or even the CFO. I didn't want them to know that the woman who had been on the Dean's List, who was sure she would become a senior manager by the age of thirty, was actually a bookkeeper, although a chief bookkeeper.

I told Daria and Inbal that I was an accountant, a job I considered more prestigious. I knew they wouldn't check, and for all they, or anyone else not in the field, knew there was no difference between a bookkeeper or an accountant or a chief accountant. Most people didn't understand the difference between a CPA and a bookkeeper, so I didn't bother to be precise and say that I was chief bookkeeper and not an accountant. I wanted to be considered the successful one in our little group, as I'd always considered myself to be.

I wanted to be envied too. I was tired of being jealous.

Within a few months, I'd established myself in the company. The CEO, the two bookkeepers who worked under me and many other workers had come to know me and my abilities. I often stayed in the office until late in the evening to finish another special report for the managers or to complete other tasks. I enjoyed taking the initiative, and I loved the appreciation I got from the CEO and the looks of respect other employees sent my way when they saw me still sitting in my office while they waved goodbye on their way home. I knew, however, that not everyone appreciated the sacrifice I had supposedly made as a young mother. One morning, when I arrived at the office, I was so pressed to use the bathroom that I went straight there without stopping at my desk. Rina, the company secretary and Deganit, the bookkeeper who handled the suppliers, entered the bathroom after me without knowing that I was in one of the stalls.

"The chief's not in yet?" Rina asked sarcastically, and I realized immediately that she was referring to me. I was aware from the very beginning that Rina couldn't stand me. It was hard for her to face the fact that a girl ten years her junior was her manager.

"I haven't seen her yet."

"Aaron told me she was here till ten o'clock yesterday evening."

"Then she's probably late because of that."

"What work could she possibly do until ten o'clock at night?"

"I have no idea," Deganit replied. "She asked me for some data yesterday before I left."

"Just trying to make an impression."

"Well, that's her right. She's a young woman, and she wants to prove herself." Deganit won a few more credit points in my book.

"She has a really small baby at home. Doesn't she

want to see her? Doesn't she need to take care of her?"

"What are you talking about? She doesn't have a little baby." Deganit pondered. "I'm pretty sure her daughter's almost two years old."

"That picture on her desk," Rina persisted, "is of a cute, smiling baby."

"That's not a current picture. She showed me a different one a few days ago on her cellphone."

"Does it seem normal to you for a mother not to have a recent photo of her child on her desk?"

"Yes," Deganit replied in a dry tone, which only made me appreciate her more.

"Well, I think it's a little weird. I mean, even if we put the picture issue aside, a two-year-old girl needs her mother. She often works late. You'd think she manages the entire world from here."

"You might be right."

"I'm definitely right. I told you from the very first moment – she's as cold as ice. Be careful around her."

Rina and Deganit's conversation aroused mixed feelings in me. On the one hand, it definitely didn't feel good to hear my parenting criticized. I was already so critical of myself to begin with. Although I didn't consider myself friends with Rina and Deganit - their age and status in the company didn't suit me and I aimed for higher social connections - it's never nice to hear that someone's so disgusted with you. On the other hand, I liked that they thought of me as an assertive and forceful woman. I knew that you couldn't get very far at work if you were nice all the time.

To look a little less abnormal, I asked Amir to take some more recent pictures of Nofar and a few weeks later, I put them on my desk in my office. Rina thought they were very nice.

I'd been with Smart Green for a year when, in January, Inbal and David had their second daughter, Adi, a little sister for Coral, who was a little more than a year old. During Inbal's first pregnancy, I'd had trouble coping with her happiness. This time, I was too busy with my new job for her happiness to bother me. Mesmerized, I watched Adi hungrily sucking at Inbal's plump breast, and I remembered how Nofar refused to nurse from mine. Coral entered the room with the clumsy run of a fourteen-month-old toddler and wrapped herself around Inbal.

"I think she's jealous," I smiled. "She probably wants some too."

"She'll get some soon."

"What will she get?" I asked, surprised.

"A breast." Inbal looked at me quizzically. She didn't understand why I was surprised.

"She's a year and two months old, and she still gets breast milk?"

"Sure."

"You're not normal."

"Why not?" she said, raising Adi to her shoulder.

"Because she's a big girl."

"She's only just over a year… and I still have milk, so why not?"

"If you say so…" I shrugged.

I thought breastfeeding a fourteen-month-old toddler was a bit extreme, but I couldn't help feeling the same old jealousy throbbing inside me again. Inbal's girls were wrapped around her from all sides and my Nofar barely wanted me at all. She didn't nurse at all, certainly not at the age of fourteen months. She was an independent little two-year-old. Everyone admired her independence, and I knew that, just as I was trying to run away from her, she ran away from me and tried to be as independent as possible in order to not need me. While I was sitting with Inbal and her daughters, Nofar chose to play with Amir and David in the living room. Her preference for Amir had always been obvious, and Amir tried to reassure me that it was just because she was daddy's little girl.

The harmony between Inbal and her daughters hurt me no less than her romantic relationship with David. I looked at Inbal's two girls and did the math in my head: Coral was four months old when Adi was conceived. I tried to remember if Amir and I had resumed having sex four months after Nofar was born. Nofar's birth was difficult, and I ended up having an episiotomy. I found it difficult to even sit for two weeks, and the pain didn't subside for months. Even after the pain abated, the frequency of sexual encounters between Amir and I was substantially reduced. Between work and taking care of Nofar, we were simply exhausted.

I was sure that Inbal and David were exhausted too, but it seemed that their parenthood, despite having two daughters, didn't affect the intimacy that existed between them. While we were all sitting in the living room, David couldn't stop stroking Inbal and looking at her with admiring eyes. I admired her too. She had patience and mothering skills I had rarely ever seen in any other mother. Her happiness and serenity rattled me. Maybe I chose the wrong approach. Maybe I should have devoted my life to Nofar and rather than staying in the office until late at night every time I could find a sitter for her. Maybe I should have stopped looking for sitters and came home early every day. Maybe I should have stopped working completely, as Inbal had.

Inbal planned to stay home at least until her youngest, who, according to her, was yet to be born, started school. Inbal could afford to put her career on hold. She was a literature teacher. Seniority wasn't as crucial in her field as it was in mine. I also had to admit to myself that I was more materialistic than her. Inbal was satisfied with the little she had. I liked to buy myself new clothes, eat in restaurants and go on luxurious vacations. For Inbal, camping on the shore of the Kinneret was a wonderful vacation while I shuddered at the very thought of sleeping in a tent. I didn't want to give up on the pleasures of life, even at the cost of having someone else taking care of my daughter.

That night, after Nofar fell asleep, I laid in bed and read a book. Amir sent a few emails and joined me in bed. I watched him as he took off his clothes. In his boxer shorts and an undershirt, it was clear that he hadn't been taking care of himself. Although he wasn't fat, he was far from the handsome officer I'd met more than ten years ago. He didn't eat well and snacked on sweets. He was addicted to caffeine, drinking at least six cups of coffee a day, which made him look perpetually tired. I, myself, didn't look the way I did on the day we met, either. I hadn't lost all my baby weight yet, but I knew I looked after myself better than he did. My mother once remarked that I should worry a little more about Amir, making sure that he ate well and watched his weight. It got on my nerves. "We don't live in the 1950s," I replied angrily. I shouldn't need to worry about my husband - he could look after himself, just like I looked after myself. Gone were the days of the man being the sole breadwinner and the wife taking care of him as she did the rest of the children. We both worked. We both provided.

David looked great. When we'd arrived at their house that day, he'd just returned from his shift and was still wearing a white undershirt, trousers and his heavy work boots. He was much sexier than I remembered him being in high school. Then, he was a teenager, and now he was a really sexy guy. His tanned, muscular body contrasted with the white undershirt he wore. Unlike Amir, he worked in a physically strenuous job. When Amir complimented him on being in such good shape, he told us that part of his workday included training in a purpose-built gym at the fire station. They had to be fit to withstand their tough work. No wonder Inbal slept with David so soon after giving birth. She was married to the live, human version of the famous statue of David.

Amir lay down next to me, and I put the book down. I began to stroke him and he smiled with pleasure. My hand went sliding under his boxers. Amir flinched and pulled my hand out.

"I'm wiped out."

"Don't you want to?"

"Sure I want to, but I'm too exhausted… let's do it tomorrow."

"Tomorrow, you're working late… you'll be exhausted then too."

"So let's plan a date for the weekend and do it properly."

"We haven't done it for almost a month."

"Right…" he said sadly.

"Aren't you attracted to me anymore?"

"Are you crazy? You know I am. I'm just tired."

"I'm sure David isn't tired, look how fast they had two girls. They're probably fucking like rabbits. And if you ask me, I look a lot better than Inbal."

He rose slightly, laid on his side, resting his head on his right hand. "I think you're much sexier than her."

"So why won't you sleep with me?"

"Of course I want to sleep with you. Now's just a busy time, so I have a little less strength in me. Three days ago, when I wanted to, you were tired... that's how it is when you have small children. We didn't invent the wheel. Everyone has less sex when they have small children."

"It's a wonder more children are born."

"True," he laughed.

"But here are Inbal and David with another baby and they look like a couple with great intimacy."

"Why do you think that?"

"I don't know. Just a hunch," I shrugged.

"I've told you a million times to stop imagining that other people have it better than you. Everyone's the same. They all have the same problems with their children, the same money issues and the same amount of sex."

"It really doesn't look that way."

"When you meet with Inbal and Daria, do you tell them about the problems you have at work? Problems with your boss?"

Daria and Inbal didn't even know that I was merely a bookkeeper, not an accountant.

"No," I replied in a whisper.

"So why do you think they'd tell you about all their troubles?" he repeated, resting his head on the pillow. "No one hangs out their dirty laundry for everyone to see," he declared.

"So what are friends for?"

"For problems more serious than a small overdraft or a child who's scared of the dark. If something really bad happened, you can be sure they'd be there for you."

I remembered how Inbal and Daria hadn't left my bedside for weeks after the accident I'd had in my youth. He was right. Maybe they were jealous of me and I just wasn't aware of it. I always had the feeling that I was the only one busy examining Daria and Asi's prosperity and Inbal and David's love life. Maybe they looked at me and found reasons to be jealous?

CHAPTER 6

In my first year at Smart Green, I blossomed professionally. Apart from the fact that I was repeatedly embarrassed by my demeaning and undignified job description, the work was interesting and challenging.

Over time, I got to know more and more employees who didn't work in my department: engineers, technicians, production workers and product designers. At first, they were all names on my payroll list, but gradually I began to associate faces with names. Being acquainted with the people I worked with while making up their paychecks every month was very difficult for me. In my mind, I saw everyone's salary flickering over his or her head. I couldn't remember the exact amount, but over time I could remember more or less each employee's wage. This troubled me. Before working at Smart Green, I'd never had to make out employee paychecks. Now, when moving through the crowds of people at work, I would constantly rank them according to the privileged information I had.

I was amazed to find that there was often no

connection between the quality of the employee and the wages he earned. There were good and loyal workers earning lower wages, while other workers doing the same job were lazy and exploitative, yet earned more. I discovered an inverse relationship between efficiency and loyalty and the ability of workers to demand their rights. My stomach turned every time my manager informed me that a lazy employee or one with a poor work ethic was getting a raise, especially when there was another employee, whom I thought was more deserving of a salary bump, who didn't get one. I was angry with my boss for not recognizing the injustices occurring in the company's salary division.

Over time, I added myself to the list of employees who were rewarded properly.

"Today, Gideon notified me about another wage adjustment," I told Amir that evening. "He gave someone from the development department an extra 2000 shekels a month."

"Very nice."

"What's nice about it? I know this man. Although he's a fairly good worker, he's not even an engineer, he's just a mechanic."

"I thought that, since Shoshana showed you that some bookkeepers have wider skills than accountants, you no longer cared about a person's job title." Amir reminded me of my predecessor.

"True, but this guy doesn't put that much effort into his work, either. I have to go through the time sheets… he does almost no overtime."

"Maybe he's just efficient?" Amir was starting to annoy me.

"I'm efficient… Gideon doesn't raise my salary like that. This guy's salary was higher than mine to begin with, and now the gap's even bigger." I sat on the couch feeling angry. Nofar approached me and handed me a paper she'd scribbled on vigorously in the last few minutes. "Good job, Nofar," I said listlessly. She looked at me, full of hope. She wanted me to admire her doodling, but it was always difficult for me to lie to her. It was just a messy scribble.

She took the drawing to Amir. "Daddy, hang it!" she ordered him in her baby voice. Amir took the doodle and praised it as if he was holding a rare work of art and then pinned it on the refrigerator with a magnet. "Go and make me another beautiful picture like this one," he said softly, and our little girl ran to her room full of motivation.

"Where was I?" I asked when we were left alone again.

"The growing gap," Amir laughed.

"It's not funny," I said angrily. "It drives me crazy that there are people who contribute less to the company than I do, yet they earn more than me."

"How do you know they contribute less?"

"Believe me, I know," I said flatly. "This guy I'm talking about works fewer hours than me. He's also less qualified, and yet he earns more."

"How old is he? Maybe he's been working there for many years?"

"He isn't much older than me, and he's only been working for Smart Green for six years."

"Only?" Amir chuckled. "He's been working there five years longer than you. That's a lot!"

"Don't forget I was buried for four years in that accounting firm. In terms of job seniority, we have almost the same experience."

"So how do you explain it?"

"That's what I keep on telling you. There's no justice! If you enter the boss's office, bang your fist on the table and threaten to leave, you get what you ask for. If you just keep quiet and accept reality as it is, you just go on getting screwed over."

"So go into Gideon's office and bang your fist on his table!"

"And if he fires me?"

"He could've fired the engineer. If he doesn't want you to go, he won't fire you."

I was afraid to go to Gideon. I didn't know what I could say to him. I'd barely been working there a year, and the first salary adjustment for workers in the company happened only after two years, certainly not less than eighteen months. I knew I wasn't going to wait another whole year, but half a year of waiting seemed like an eternity too.

When I started working on payroll, it never occurred to me it would entail such emotional difficulty. I didn't see workers; I saw numbers. I could rate all the workers from the most expensive to the least expensive, just like grades pinned on the bulletin board in the principal's office. Next to each name was a number. The higher the number, the more that person was to be respected. That analogy between pay scales and school grades ran through my mind again and again. During my studies at university, my ranking gave me confidence. I wasn't always in first place, but I always knew that the list was realistic. The best student received the highest score. The employee list was very different. Those who received the highest salary weren't necessarily the best employees, at least not in my opinion, and it bothered me. It was more than just the financial reward. The payroll was a simplistic way for me to rate the company's employees.

I didn't like my position. I thought I deserved to be ranked higher.

A year and two months after I started working at Smart Green, I knew I couldn't continue with the way things were. I decided to go to Gideon, even though my contract stated clearly that I wouldn't be considered for a raise until I'd worked there for two years.

I decided to take a chance.

I entered Gideon's office after practicing my speech for a week. He smiled at me and asked what I wanted.

"I want to talk about something personal," I said.

"Please," he gestured to the chair opposite him. "Come and sit down."

I had a feeling he thought I was going to tell him I was pregnant.

"I'm not pregnant," I blurted out immediately. "At least, not as far as I know," I smiled.

"That's fine," he said with a look of appreciation. "You know that Smart Green respects mothers. You must have heard that Deganit, who works with you, returned from a nine-month maternity leave just before you started your job."

"Yes, I heard."

"But you're not pregnant, so what did you want to tell me?"

"Gideon," I cleared my throat. I didn't want my voice to tremble. I wanted to sound as assertive as I could. "I think you know how much I enjoy working for this company." He nodded. "This job is everything I dreamed of and more. I'm learning a lot and enjoy helping in any way that my training and experience allows."

"I'm very pleased with you too," he said immediately. I knew he was very pleased with me. He never hid it and made sure to praise me with compliments and reassurance.

"But there are two things that bother me. Really bother me."

"What?" he asked a worried tone.

"The first issue is my job description. In many other companies, what I do is considered the job of an accountant and not the work of a bookkeeper."

"*Chief* bookkeeper!" he immediately corrected.

"And I think, as a result," I continued my speech, "my salary is inappropriate for my role." He looked at me, shocked, but I knew I had to finish what I came there to say. "I don't know why my role's entitled chief bookkeeper [I made sure to add the 'Chief'] and not an accountant." The truth is that I had a pretty good idea why my job title wasn't 'accountant.' The salary of an accountant would be almost double. "Maybe it's because Shoshana, my predecessor, was a bookkeeper by profession." I tried to come up with a logical reason for Gideon.

"You're doing exactly the same work Shoshana did."

"I have to tell you that Shoshana's knowledge wasn't that of an ordinary bookkeeper, or even of a chief bookkeeper," I hastened to add. "And since I came here, I've added quite a bit to the content of management reports, additional material that Shoshana didn't put in."

I watched Gideon. His gaze was frozen. I didn't know how to interpret it. I continued, as I'd practiced. "I know it's not fair to use the knowledge I'm privy to about other employees' wages, but I think it's just not fair that I earn, just as an example, four thousand shekels less than Ofer Kaduri."

Gideon frowned. "Hasn't Ofer just had a 2000 shekel raise?"

"Yes," I replied passionately, "and he's a practical engineer. He doesn't even have a college degree like I do."

"So you think you deserve an extra 4000 shekels?"

Honestly, I thought I deserved more than Ofer Kaduri, but I was embarrassed to say the exact amount I thought I deserved. "Something like that," I said, and I tilted my head from side to side, as if trying to weigh the money in my head. Gideon checked something on the computer. I thought it was a good sign, that maybe he was calculating how much he should give me.

He turned away from his computer, looked straight at me and said in the angriest voice I have ever heard, "I have to tell you, you are *rude*!" He swallowed and continued. "*So* rude! You compare yourself to Ofer Kaduri or Shoshana? How dare you?"

I hunched down in my chair and he continued. "Ofer Kaduri has been working here for six years and this was his first significant raise. The raise you're asking for would bring you, more or less, to Shoshana's wage level, and she worked here for more than fifteen years! How do you even dare compare yourself to these two workers? While we're at it, how dare you use other employees' salary data to your personal ends?"

I felt tears welling in my eyes. I couldn't answer him because I knew that if I opened my mouth, I'd cry.

"You think I don't know your wages here are about fifty percent higher than you earned with your last employer? You came here and dramatically improved your working conditions and signed an agreement that stated you wouldn't be getting a salary review for two years... and now you want to break the rules?"

"I don't want to break the rules," I managed to say without bursting into tears.

"Maybe you don't, but I would *really* like to fire you right now!"

I was shocked. I couldn't believe the conversation had come this far. Now, without even uttering another word, I burst into tears. Gideon was stunned. Like many men, he didn't know how to respond to a crying woman.

"I'm sorry," I said, sobbing. "It was bothering me, and I thought it would be best to talk to you... It was beginning to interfere with my work." Gideon got up from his chair. I was afraid he was going to throw me out, but he went to the dresser behind him and took out a pack of tissues for me.

He stood next to me, folded his arms, leaned on his desk and said calmly, "I apologize. Maybe I overreacted a little, but you really made me very angry. I do want you to come to me when you have a problem and not bottle things up, but I also expect you to use your discretion - and you absolutely did *not* use it today." I nodded in agreement, even though I still thought I was right. "I'm very happy with you and your work, and I believe you can have a great future in this company. I'm also sure that, if you keep at it, your wages will go up, but all in good time."

I left the room. Rina, his secretary, couldn't fail to miss my red eyes and immediately picked up her phone and dialed, probably to announce the hot gossip to one of my bookkeepers. I didn't want to let the story escalate, and I left the building. Across the road was a small café. I sat down and ordered a cup of coffee. I drank it slowly, to calm down and let the tears stop before I went back to the office. I thought to myself that maybe I did over exaggerate and some of my demands were not legitimate after only a year with the company, but Gideon's reaction blew me away. I was really offended. Is a request for a higher salary reason enough to threaten an employee with dismissal? I was sure it wasn't. If I hadn't needed the job and the salary, I'd have gone right up there and collected my things.

When I got home and cried into Amir's shoulder, he was forced to agree with me that Gideon's response was a bit extreme. However, he reminded me that he thought I should wait patiently until at least the end of my second year with Smart Green, and he also thought that I should stop making comparisons between the employees, but compare my salary with that of colleagues in other companies.

"But I'm the chief bookkeeper, not an accountant," I said tearfully.

"Tell me," Amir said quietly, stroking me softly. "Is there anything you're missing?"

"Yeah, I'm not an accountant!" I answered immediately with bitterness.

"Let the title go," he said almost angrily and then returned to speaking calmly. "I mean do you lack for anything?"

"I could use more money..."

"I don't lack for anything. We do pretty well for our age. We both have stable jobs, and I think you enjoy your work very much. How many people can say that?"

"I don't know," I shrugged. I didn't like the logic in Amir's words. I wanted to wallow in self-pity.

"Not many, I assure you. You do this to yourself all the time, Rose. You compare yourself with others instead of focusing on what you have. Stop imagining others have it better all the time, and start enjoying and appreciating what you do have."

He was right. But it was hard for me to get off my high horse. I'd been up there for so long. I found it hard to get my feet back on the ground.

CHAPTER 7

Four months after Adi, Inbal and David's second daughter, was born, Daria and Asi also had a daughter, Shira. According to my calculations, Daria became pregnant immediately after Inbal announced her second pregnancy. Like always, she didn't want to be left behind.

Daria didn't miss the chance to flaunt her wealth and the fact that she'd managed to get back in shape in less than two months, so she organized a lavish party to show off the baby and her figure. After Inbal and I finished admiring her remarkable weight loss, her revealing dress and the flashy pink decorations of the venue, she led us to our tables, but not before she had us swear to "try everything" from the buffet, although we had no doubt that she wouldn't put even one grain of rice in her own mouth. We couldn't sit quietly for more than two minutes: David and Amir were busy chasing Nofar and little Coral while Inbal and I couldn't exchange even one sentence without baby Adi bothering us. When Adi began to scream incessantly, our fragmented conversation ended officially, and Inbal took

Adi out to calm her down. I sat and played listlessly with my iPhone.

"Didn't you study accounting at the University of Tel Aviv?" the girl sitting across the table asked me in a cautious tone.

"Yes," I replied, looking up. She seemed familiar to me.

"I knew I recognized you!" She smiled a satisfied smile. "My husband and I also did accounting in Tel Aviv. Maybe you know my husband? He's just running around after Guy, our son. When did you graduate?"

"I graduated in 2004, but then I did an extra year. How about you?"

"Lior graduated in 2002, and I finished up in 2003. I think we did a course together… perhaps it was Managerial Accountancy?"

"Maybe. You finished your extra year or your degree in 2003?"

"I didn't complete the extra year." She rose from her chair and moved to sit next to me. "I'm not a CPA."

"Really?"

"I did a degree in law and accounting, and I chose to specialize in law."

"So you're a lawyer?"

"Yes, both of us are."

"Oh. I studied economics and accounting and specialized in accounting."

"Lior and I debated the matter and in the end we chose to specialize in law, but I don't regret it."

"I don't regret my choice either," I said. In truth I wasn't sure whether I did or not, though I hadn't had the option to specialize in law.

"We didn't throw away our accounting studies." She smiled. "After I finished my internship, we went to New

York for a year and got our master's in management, so it was very helpful."

"Very nice," I said, feeling a green cloud of jealousy began to hover over me.

"How do you know Daria?" she inquired.

"We're childhood friends. How about you?"

"My son's in the same kindergarten as Roy."

"So you live in Daria and Asi's neighborhood?"

"Just two buildings over," she said. She spotted Lior from afar and signaled him over. "Lior, you remember..." She looked at me and she remembered that she'd forgotten to ask my name.

"Rose Yanku. Actually, in school I was still Rose Lerner."

"Rose Lerner," she finished the sentence.

Lior approached, a golden-haired boy bundled up in his hands. "Hello," he smiled at me. He looked at me and smiled sheepishly. "The truth is, I don't really remember you."

I didn't recognize him either.

"Rose studied a year below me and two below you, maybe that's why."

The blond child didn't let Lior join the conversation, and we were left alone again.

"How many children do you have?" she asked.

"One daughter." I pointed out Nofar, who was watching a clown modeling balloons with interest. "Nofar."

"We also have only one child," she said sadly. "Excuse me for asking, but do you have problems?"

"What problems?"

"You know..." she stammered, "fertility problems..."

"Why?" I looked at her, stunned, "I'm only thirty, and I have one child already."

"Oh, sorry," she said, embarrassed. "She just seems to be a big girl and you don't look at all pregnant," she tried to flatter me.

"I don't understand," I said. I was confused by her slightly embarrassing questions.

"Forgive me," she said, and I saw that she was on the verge of tears. "It's just that almost everyone I know is having their second child."

"So?" I asked nonchalantly, as if I never compared myself to others. "Just because everyone has another child, I need to as well?"

"Absolutely not," she smiled and blew her nose. "If I didn't really want another baby, it wouldn't bother me at all." I looked at her with empathy. I knew how she felt. I'd never longed for another child, but I knew how it felt to not get what you want. In recent years, I always felt like I was chasing happiness and yet always unable to attain it.

"You must forgive me," she said. "I barely know you, and here I am dumping all my troubles on you."

"It's okay," I smiled. "Sometimes it's easier to talk to strangers."

"Yes," she laughed, "but you're not really a stranger."

We continued to talk and laugh. The conversation flowed, mainly because we began to talk about our professors and classmates. It was hard to say goodbye, and we decided to meet again for a breezy brunch at the weekend.

"I saw you were sitting with Aya Steinfeld the entire time." Daria called me the next day and proved for the umpteenth time that she never missed anything.

"She's very nice."

"They're a ridiculously successful pair," Daria hurried

to update me.

"Who?"

"She and her husband."

"Yes... she told me they're lawyers."

"Right. What did you talk about for so long?"

"We were at school together."

"Why would you have been studying together? She studied Law."

"They studied both law and accounting."

"Really? You can learn it together?"

"Yes, the two subjects really overlap."

"Her husband's a partner in a firm that specializes in tax law, to the best of my knowledge, so it makes sense."

"He's a partner?" I asked in amazement. "How old is he?"

"He's thirty-five and, to my knowledge, she's thirty-three." Now I understood why she was so stressed about parenthood - they were a little older than Amir and me.

"He's still very young to be a partner."

"Extremely young! I told you they were a successful pair. I don't know exactly who she works for, but I heard that she's working for one of the most prestigious firms in the country. She goes off to meetings in the Knesset in Jerusalem."

"Why?"

"I don't know... she represents very big companies who probably deal with the Knesset members and give them a hard time."

"Wow!"

"Yeah, they're a very impressive couple. I keep trying to have Roy and their son play together, but their son's too laid back for my son," she giggled.

"We'll be seeing them this weekend," I put in. "We'll see how Nofar gets along with the Crown Prince."

"They have a fabulous house. You're sure to be impressed."

"Good for them."

"It really is good for them. Most people here in our neighborhood inherited their money, but they really earned theirs. She's originally from Kiryat Gat, and I think he's from Netanya."

I didn't know if she told me all this to make me jealous, but I was flooded with negative emotions again. My background was much more privileged than those who grew up in a remote, developing town, but I didn't see how we could possibly buy an apartment in an upscale neighborhood in northern Tel Aviv in the coming years. Aya, Lior and I had started at the same point, educationally. The three of us studied at the same school, I was even an outstanding student, none of us had any connections or a rich daddy and yet they'd been able to steer themselves higher than me. Maybe I'd made a mistake by choosing to be a CPA. Maybe I should have gone to law school. I didn't feel I was missing anything material in my life. Amir and I made a good living, and we lived in a cute apartment (with a choking mortgage). We lived the Israeli dream. But for me, this dream was too trite and didn't aim high enough. I felt that I should be achieving more. My mother told me that I'd always been like that, even before the accident. She and my father tried occasionally to moderate my need to be constantly in first place, to no avail. In my childhood and youth, the disappointments were smaller and the successes were easier to reach, but as time passed, it was harder for me to reach that summit, and I had to feel the bitter taste of disappointment again and again. The sense of 'what if' paralyzed me once again, as it had when I found out I was pregnant with Nofar.

I nearly cried off our invite to Aya and Lior's house; I didn't want to see their incredible home and their perfect life. Aya texted me the day before to make sure we hadn't forgotten our date, because she was looking forward to it and had a really cute surprise for me. I had no excuse, and I was also curious.

When we got there the next day, Amir couldn't hide his astonishment at the luxury apartment. He embarrassed me a little with his childlike enthusiasm, as if he'd left behind a pauper's house and this was his first encounter with a decorated apartment.

"What's this surprise you promised me?" I asked Aya as we sat down.

"Oh, yes!" She jumped up and went to the cupboard in the dining area. "I put it here," she said, scrambling through papers and envelopes. "Here it is!" She looked pleased and returned with a picture in her hand.

"All that talk about school conjured up a sense of nostalgia in me, and I began looking at pictures and look what I found." She handed me the picture.

The picture was of her and Lior holding their certificates in their hands and smiling to the camera. I strained my eyes, and I realized that it was the Dean's List certificate given out to students by the accounting faculty. I studied the photo and recognized myself standing a few feet away with my certificate, probably smiling at Amir, who was taking a picture of me at the same time.

"When was this taken?" I inquired.

"The ceremony of 2002. It was the last time we were on the Dean's List."

"You were on the Dean's List every year?"

"Lior was. I didn't make it in my last year. I understand that, according to the picture, you were a regular at these ceremonies."

"I got two," I said coyly.

"Aya showed you the picture she found?" Lior and Amir returned from their tour of the flat.

"Yes." I smiled and showed Amir the image.

"So you were also on the Dean's List." Lior looked at me in a manner I assumed he reserved for people he respected.

"Yes." I smiled.

"Where do you work?" Lior took interest.

"I'm an accountant at Smart Green." I exchanged glances with Amir. He didn't like me lying about my job, but I didn't want this successful pair to view me as a failure.

"I haven't heard of it, have you?" Lior asked Aya.

"No."

"It's a fairly small company that handles the development of ecological products for industry."

"Sounds interesting."

"Very."

"I recently handled a case for a company that deals in wastewater recycling… ACMS. Have you heard of them, by any chance?"

"Actually, yes. I think they had a small project with us."

Lior smiled, but he couldn't engage with the conversation beyond what he said himself. We forced our smiles. I found it difficult to open up with Lior as I did with Aya.

"Maybe you guys should go down to the garden with Nofar and Guy?" Aya suggested after a few minutes of meaningless sentences and awkward silences. "The garden's just had a makeover. It's really cute now."

"Great idea!" Amir immediately jumped up. He was

bored.

After Lior and Amir went out with the kids, Aya and I could talk calmly and openly.

"You guys met in school?" I was curious. I knew that the more I learned about this amazing couple, the more my jealousy would grow, but I wanted to get to know her, merely for the chance of learning something about her life that would lessen my envy.

"Yes," she smiled. "We noticed that we kept on meeting both at the law faculty and the business management faculty."

"Nice, I don't know many couples who met in the faculty."

"I don't either."

"Then you studied together in New York?"

"Yes, it was an amazing year," she said, her voice filled with longing.

"You went there after you finished your internship?"

"Yes."

"I wish I'd been able to do something like that, but I got pregnant right after my internship," I confessed in a voice full of bitterness.

"Nofar wasn't planned?" Aya asked, puzzled.

"Not really," I smiled sheepishly.

"I wish."

"To have an unplanned pregnancy?" I asked in surprise and hope sparked in my heart that maybe Aya was jealous of me.

"To get pregnant without waiting so long. It took us three years to conceive the first time and now we've been trying for a year already."

"But Guy's still young."

"He's two, and I'm nearing thirty-five. It's not so easy for me to get pregnant as is, and the older I get, the harder it becomes." She looked at me with sad eyes. "You're not trying to get pregnant again?"

"No."

"You don't talk about it?"

"Sometimes."

A few weeks ago, when we celebrated Leil Ha-Seder with Amir's extended family, his aunt had asked him with typical tactlessness if we had fertility problems. Her daughters had bundles of children, one after the other, and the fact that we had a three year old and there were no signs of a second child was sufficient reason to suspect that we suffered from infertility. The seemingly innocent question had released a cork in Amir and, from that moment on, he never stopped bothering me about it. He took the trouble to remind me repeatedly that my fertility would gradually lessen over the years, and that children needed siblings and playmates. Any announcement of a second pregnancy by a friend or relative would result in a long and depressing conversation in which Amir went back over the variety of reasons for extending our family. I vehemently continued to refuse to contribute my womb for the demographic efforts of the Yanku family.

Aya confessed, "For me, I feel like it's completely taking over my life. I have no control over it, and there's so much uncertainty... It's very difficult for me."

I thought the opposite. I had lost control of my life because I gave birth to a child and not because I couldn't bring a child into the world.

"Look on the bright side, Aya," I tried to comfort her. "With two children, it'd be very difficult to advance your career."

"Believe me, I'd give up my career. I have no doubt that I wouldn't have gotten this far if I'd been able to get pregnant when I wanted, but my entire career has been a series of accidental opportunities... nothing was planned."

Again, I thought our experiences were completely opposite: she wanted a child and had a career; I wanted a career and had gotten a child. The difference between us was that she would eventually have both - a child and a career - while I didn't have a career and was far from being Mother of the Year.

"I envy girls like you, who suddenly discover they're pregnant," she said candidly. I envied her, her remarkable career, her magnificent home and all the patience and love she lavished on her son. It was difficult for me to express it in words. Perhaps she could express it because her jealousy was more legitimate.

After that meeting, we kept in touch. I found it hard to understand why I tolerated this relationship, which I'd recognized as clearly unhealthy for me from the very first moment. Lior and Aya's success, especially since they'd started exactly where I started, drove me nuts. They were a couple of successful lawyers who lived in a luxury apartment, and I was far behind them with my lousy job and my little apartment with the endless mortgage. Aya was the one making sure our newfound friendship didn't fade away, but I didn't make a point of steering clear of her, as I should have. I guess it gave me a perverse pleasure to see Aya's difficulty conceiving. Despite all her success, she had difficulties in an area that I managed without any effort.

CHAPTER 8

Two months after I met Aya, I was pregnant again. I don't know if it was the constant preoccupation with the subject of Aya's fertility, or my desire to beat her in something that made me surrender to Amir's incessant requests to try for another child. I felt insecure at work after the difficult conversation with Gideon, and I felt it wasn't the right time to take a break from my career, but I wanted to feel that, in one aspect at least, I was better than Aya. The last time I got pregnant without even noticing, so I figured that this time wouldn't be difficult either. Indeed, I got pregnant in our first month.

The two stripes that graced the test stick indicator made my face light up. Amir was flooded with joy, both because of the upcoming pregnancy and because this time, unlike the last, I seemed to be happy with the pregnancy. I couldn't admit to anyone the real secret — that the horrible reason for my happiness was that I'd finally succeeded in something that Aya had failed at. I'd won the little contest I'd made up in my overworked mind.

I knew that Aya hadn't boasted about her triumphs to make me jealous, but I still waited impatiently for my first ultrasound. Amir thought I wanted to see our little fetus, but the sad truth was that I wanted medical confirmation of the pregnancy so that I could run and tell Aya. I wanted her to be jealous.

Three days before the long-awaited ultrasound, I was sitting in my office going through bank statements. In the two weeks since I'd found out I was pregnant, my work at Green Smart had become easier on me. Nothing bothered me as it once had, not the salaries of the other employees, not Gideon's angry glances (he hadn't quite forgotten our meeting), not the dozens of requests from customers and suppliers that came my way every day. I felt I'd won. I was able to get pregnant. And it was so easy! I was a fertile woman. There was something I was good at, very good, in fact. I started to fantasize about taking my maternity leave. I decided to take at least six months. This time, I wanted to experience motherhood. I felt that, this time, the pregnancy was something I wanted and so it would all be different. This time, the child would love me. I wanted to make things right in my life. The first time I got pregnant, the pregnancy came as a surprise ,and I felt that it halted my life. This time, the pregnancy was planned and desired, and so I hoped my motherhood experience would be a better one.

As I was thinking about it, I noticed a change on some banking documentation and started to look into it. Suddenly, I felt a sharp griping pain in my stomach. When I was pregnant with Nofar, I'd had some abdominal discomfort, sometimes extremely strong, but it was mainly toward the end of pregnancy when Nofar kicked me. I sat there in the office, hoping it was nothing, but when the pain intensified I realized something was very wrong. I ran to the bathroom, took off my panties and let out a terrifying scream. My underwear was soaked in blood.

I ran to my desk, picked up my bag and simply fled to my car. I didn't bother even to stamp my timecard on the way out. Rina looked at me with a stunned expression, and I knew my dramatic exit would be reported to all the relevant people within seconds. I called Amir on the way.

"I'm in a meeting," he whispered.

"I'm bleeding!" I yelled. "I'm having terrible pains."

"Wait a second," he said and I realized he'd left the conference room. "What happened?" he said in a worried voice.

"I felt a strange pain, so I went to the bathroom... I... I'm bleeding badly."

"Where are you now?"

"On my way to the ER."

"I'm on my way," he said and hung up.

In the ER, they found an amniotic sac without a fetus, but couldn't find a pulse. They tried to calm me down by saying that it was early in the pregnancy, so it was quite possible not to see anything and it could be a pregnancy hemorrhage, but I knew.

I'd miscarried.

The doctors recommended that I wait, let my body get over the trauma, but I went into a frenzy.

I had to get pregnant again. I didn't know if I was trying to compensate myself or if I was still in competition with Aya. I didn't tell her about the miscarriage. No one knew except Amir and my parents. I didn't want to be seen as a failure. Amir and my mother tried to explain to me that miscarrying at this stage of the pregnancy was common and that I shouldn't get too shaken up, but their words fell on deaf ears. I couldn't listen to anyone. I felt that the only easy thing in my life had suddenly become impossible.

At first, Amir refused to have sex with me. He couldn't understand my obsession with getting pregnant again, but when he realized how much it meant to me, he gave in. We were never sex addicts; we liked having relaxed and enjoyable sex at times that suited us. Now the sex was mechanical, depressing and sometimes painful and unpleasant. Several times, Amir had trouble reaching his climax. I forgot that sex could even be pleasurable.

Two months after my miscarriage, Aya sent me a picture of a pregnancy test with two lines on it. She didn't know I was trying to get pregnant, that I had, and that I'd lost the baby. I'm sure if she'd known, she wouldn't have sent the picture. Only someone who's experienced such frustration knows how difficult it is to be happy for others in that situation. She wrote that, since she'd driven me crazy about it, she thought I should know about the pregnancy before she even told her mother. I told her I was happy for her.

Mostly, I was glad that I didn't need to speak. Tears choked my throat. The picture of that positive test paralyzed me. That day, I could think of nothing else but Aya's two lines. I was so distracted that I forgot to go to a meeting with Gideon and an insurance agent. Gideon had to ask Rina to call me in and she obviously relished every moment she spent proving my lack of concentration. I sat in the meeting, but heard nothing. Gideon and the agent laughed, then debated and talked while I sat and stared into the distance. At one point, Gideon asked me to check something the agent mentioned. I nodded, even though I'd no idea what they were talking about. When the agent left, Gideon asked me to stay.

"Is everything all right?" he asked.

"Yes," I replied in a voice that lack credibility.

"You don't seem very focused. I don't think you were with us at the meeting at all."

"True," I looked down. "I'm not feeling so good."

"I'll ask again," he said empathetically. "Is everything all right? Rina told me that a few weeks ago, you stormed out of the office very upset."

I considered telling him about the miscarriage. By law, I could have stayed home, sick, for a week, but I didn't. I thought that could possibly play in my favor. In the end, I decided it would be better not to have everyone know that I was trying to conceive.

"My daughter wasn't feeling well," I lied and felt bad for using my child to lie.

"And now?"

"Just a headache."

I knew he guessed I was pregnant or that I had miscarried. In recent years, I hadn't been able to say I was nauseous without everyone congratulating me. I preferred him guessing it rather than knowing it for certain. He was just another person who didn't know what I was going through, just like Aya, who missed no opportunity to update me on her pregnancy. I was sickened to realize that, whenever she texted or called me, I wished her pregnancy would end in a miscarriage. Before each checkup she had, I prayed that the test would show an abnormality. I wanted us to return to the same starting point.

But, contrary to all my prayers, Aya's pregnancy developed properly, and she flourished day by day. She blossomed, and I shriveled. I fell apart every month when my period arrived again, and Amir had to be there to pick up the pieces. For half a year, I forced him to have sex that lacked both desire and pleasure, and I scolded him whenever he found it difficult to perform. The worst day was when Aya informed me that her latest ultrasound had picked up the baby's pulse.

According to my calculations, I was ovulating that same day. Amir arrived home late, even though I'd asked him not to be late. He had a conference call with New York, and he couldn't make it home early. He tiptoed into the house. I woke up in spite of his efforts to be quiet and immediately scolded him.

"I'm ovulating today!" I declared.

"Hello to you too." He tried to calm me down.

"This isn't the time for a lesson in pleasantry," I said angrily. "I told you to get here early because I'm ovulating."

"I'm sorry, really. I couldn't get out sooner."

"You've been driving me crazy about getting pregnant for months and now that I'm on board, you don't make any serious effort."

"You're right," he said in a whisper, reminding me that Nofar could wake up. "But, in any case, I don't feel so well. I told you already."

"If you had the strength to go to work, then you can also put a little effort in for me," I whispered in a way that was practically a shout. "I mean, for us," I corrected myself immediately.

He exhaled and looked at me in despair. "Okay," he said. "I just want to eat something small. I'm starved."

I went into the shower to freshen up a bit. I saw the messy woman looking back at me in the mirror and nearly cried. No wonder he didn't want to sleep with me.

I looked like a weirdo with messy hair and wrinkled clothes. I undressed and got into the shower. I decided to be pretty for Amir. I scrubbed myself and shampooed my hair. When I finished, I dabbed scented creams on myself and combed my wet hair. When I went back into the bedroom, Amir was already snoring on his side of the bed with his clothes still on. I jumped on him with delight. He woke up in confusion.

"What are you doing?" he shouted in alarm.

"What do you think?" I chuckled with amusement, hoping he'd play along.

He didn't. His startled face was replaced by an angry one. "I told you, I don't feel well! Why are you jumping on me like that?"

It was my turn to change my facial expression from amused to insulted. "I'm just trying to get you in the mood."

"I really don't have the energy," he said, trying to smile.

"You don't need much," I said firmly, ignoring his rejection and working toward my goal.

Before Amir could object again, I unzipped his pants and reached inside. After a few minutes of effort I had to accept nothing was going to happen. My egg wasn't going to meet any sperm tonight. I lay down next to Amir, exhausted and disappointed. Amir turned to me with his trousers rolled down to his knees. I looked at his limp penis gloomily.

"Sorry," he said. "I told you I wasn't feeling well."

"But I'm ovulating today... we're going to lose an entire month just because your work's more important to you than us."

"That's not true."

"It absolutely is..." I said and started to cry.

He pulled his pants up, reached over to me and started to gently caress my face. "Everything's okay. This is really nothing to cry about. We're not in any race." The problem was that I *was* in a race, a race he was unaware of and I had no doubt that, if he'd been aware of it, he'd have nothing to do with it.

I finally managed to get pregnant. About six months after the miscarriage, when Aya was in her second trimester, I got to see the long-awaited two stripes on my pregnancy test. I waved the test stick like a trophy. I'd done it!

Amir was still sleeping when I did the test. I jumped on him with joy. "Look!" I said happily.

Amir looked at the stick and smiled sleepily. "We're having a baby!" he said.

"I'm pregnant!" I corrected him and then realized that I'd been so busy chasing the pregnancy for the last six months that I'd just forgotten that the goal was a baby, not a pregnancy.

Waiting for the first ultrasound was nerve wracking. Last time, I'd miscarried right before the first scan, but this time I passed the test and we heard a pulse. Amir was happy; he was about to be a father again. I was happy; I had a healthy pregnancy. The black cloud hovering over me began to disperse.

"We're also expecting," I informed Aya, in one of the few conversations I initiated in those months.

"Wow!" she said happily. "How long have you known?"

"A month and a half now."

"And only now you're telling me?" She sounded offended.

"I wanted to be sure."

"You weren't sure?" she chuckled. "All you have to do is smell your husband and you automatically get pregnant."

I didn't want to correct her. I wanted her to think that, at least in one respect, I was better than her.

"Well..." I stammered, looking for an answer, "Amir asked me not to say anything... his family's very superstitious."

"Really?" she laughed. "I wouldn't have guessed."

"Trust me... they really are..." I joined her laughter.

"Then we'll be on maternity leave together!" she said, delighted.

"Won't you have finished your maternity leave by the time I give birth?"

"You think I'd only take three months off? I've been waiting for this child for so long, I want to be with him as much as possible."

"Aren't you worried about your career?"

"Absolutely not," she said without even pausing to think, and again, I envied her determination and certainty of her priorities in life. I wasn't sure if I wanted to extend my maternity leave. I felt my status in the company was unstable. I was afraid I wouldn't have a place to return to after my maternity leave and, the more I extended it, the more likely it was that my replacement would take my place. Rina never stopped bragging about her nephew passing the accounting council tests, though with a barely passing grade, and I was afraid she'd stick him in my office and then make sure he stayed there. I knew I had to get someone to replace me, omeone to have control over.

I found my candidate months in advance: Erez, the intern who had replaced me in the accounting firm where I had once worked and came on a quarterly basis to prepare the financial statements. The fact that he was an intern was my security blanket. He had to return to the accountants' office and finish his internship. On the one hand, he knew the case and the company because he prepared the quarterly and annual reports, but on the other hand, because I spoke with him often, I knew that my job didn't interest him. He aspired to be a CFO, not an accountant. The routine work bored him, and he wanted to do business. I chuckled to myself about his grandiose ambitions. He was just an intern and already he aspired to reach the highest office our training would allow. I tried to explain to him that financial officer positions weren't just waiting out there for beginner accountants to snatch them up, but he was determined.

When I finished my first trimester, I went to Gideon and told him about the pregnancy and the due date. He immediately said we needed to find a replacement for me.

"There's still some time," I said. I didn't want to tell him who I'd picked out to be my replacement. I didn't want him to know how important my job was to me. I wanted him to think Erez was just a fleeting thought that passed through my mind and not a stand-in I'd preplanned way in advance.

"True, but you hold a senior and central position here," he said, and I thought how, when I have to take time off, my job suddenly becomes a senior and central one.

"I'll think of something," I promised. "I just finished the first trimester of my pregnancy. I don't want people to know yet and if we start looking for a temporary replacement, everybody will start talking."

"Okay," Gideon replied reluctantly.

"Gideon..." I began hesitantly because he already

knew about the pregnancy, and I knew there was no point in hiding the miscarriage. "You remember the time I ran out of the office a few months ago?"

"Yes."

"I had a miscarriage that day." I looked down. The truth was that the memory wasn't particularly painful, but I wanted Gideon to think it was a very sensitive issue for me.

"I figured," he said softly. "My wife also had several miscarriages, and I had a feeling."

"That's why I don't want anybody except you to know until mid-pregnancy."

"Okay," he said in a fatherly voice that reminded me of my first year working here, when I felt like his protégé.

"I promise I'll look for someone discreetly."

"I'm counting on you," he smiled.

Three weeks later, I managed to speak to Erez, who was happy to be free of the drab office routine, and offered the idea to Gideon. Gideon thought it was a great idea. He called Reuben, who worked opposite him in the accounting firm, and asked if it was possible to have Erez work with us for several months. Reuben explained to Gideon that Erez would, in fact, continue to work for the accounting firm, but would be subcontracted to Smart Green, so his internship period wouldn't be affected.

For me, this arrangement was perfect. Erez wasn't even working for the company. I felt safe to go on maternity leave and then return to my role.

CHAPTER 9

Tom was born in August 2011, at the beginning of the ninth month of pregnancy. The contractions began when I was sitting with Erez, explaining how to prepare the paychecks. Erez asked something, and an intense pain shot through my body. He looked stunned. He was single and had never had anything to do with childbirth. Despite his panic, he helped me get to my car and drove me to the hospital, where he was replaced by Amir.

My pregnancy with Nofar began easily and ended with difficulties. This time, I had the opposite experience: it was harder to get pregnant, but the delivery was over within hours. Despite being born almost a month ahead of schedule, Tom was a cute, chubby baby. This time, I wasn't exhausted and when the nurse handed him to me, I embraced him warmly. I felt I'd be a better mother this time around. Unlike Nofar, Tom nursed from me greedily. I enjoyed nursing him; I felt we'd established a connection he would never have with anyone else in the world.

Nofar came to meet her younger brother a day after he was born. Tom was nursing when she came in with Amir. She walked toward me hesitantly, reaching out her hand to touch Tom.

"Don't touch him," I shouted in alarm. I didn't know if she'd washed her hands thoroughly.

Nofar, frightened by my shout, ran to Amir, who looked at me, stunned.

"Nofari," I said softly, "you can touch the baby. You just need to wash your hands really well first. He's very small and isn't allowed to get sick."

She didn't want to get close to him anymore.

Although the delivery was easy and the hospital stay was pleasant, the timing was bad. I thought that I'd give birth at the very end of Nofar's kindergarten vacation, so I'd have some peace and quiet until the afternoon came. But once I got back from the hospital, I didn't have a minute's rest. This wasn't a vacation.

For four years, I hadn't been able to identify a single feature that connected Nofar with me, but once Tom was born, I knew she was my daughter. Jealousy seared her soul. She did everything to get my attention, which was primarily given to little Tom. The majority of attention she managed to get was down to bad behavior. She would intentionally pick on Tom or get up to some kind of mischief. She'd wait for Tom to fall asleep so I'd be available and then smear herself with chocolate, paint the walls, break a dish or simply burst into inexplicable tears. More than once I couldn't help myself, and I'd shout at her to be more careful. Obviously, my shouting did no good and Tom would wake up sobbing. I'd just given birth, but couldn't rest at all.

In my fantasy, I saw myself walking with my baby in green gardens, sitting at the end of the boulevard café, drinking iced coffee. I imagined how I'd use my mornings to clean up the house and prepare nutritious meals for Nofar and Amir. In practice, Amir would return each evening to a neglected home, sobbing children and an exhausted wife. It was a very busy period for him at work, and he rarely managed to get home early. Every time I called and yelled at him to help me, he answered in a weak voice that he couldn't just get up and go. Recently, his company had been implementing massive layoffs, and he was afraid to leave early.

I hated going out with both children. Any outing was a tiresome project that demanded lots of organizing and made me lose my desire to see the light of day. When Tom was a little over two months old, Inbal insisted I go visit her with Nofar and Tom. I'd always been spellbound by Inbal's parenting skills, but now I was a mother of two myself. I looked at her conduct with her two little girls in open admiration. Coral wasn't yet three years old and little Adi was a little over eighteen months. They ran around her constantly, and she made sure to respond to every question and request with admirable patience.

When we arrived, she got out some ingredients and invited Nofar to join them making chocolate chip cookies. Nofar savored every moment, eagerly mixing ingredients in a bowl and then forming small balls of dough that eventually went in the oven and turned, after a short period of baking, into sweet cookies. Inbal didn't seem to worry about the mess the girls made in the kitchen or the fact that Adi lost her concentration very quickly and began to take out different dishes from the cupboard and play with them. She just played with the girls with delight and harmony. I wanted to be like that too, but every time Nofar didn't have something to do and I didn't want her to watch TV, I sent her to play with her dolls or draw something.

A few days later I decided to also do a cooking workshop with Nofar. I searched the Internet for a suitable recipe and decided to make cupcakes. The beginning was promising; Nofar, who wasn't used to spending quality time with me, was thrilled with the activity I'd planned. She looked curiously at the tin that I'd bought especially for making the cupcakes and thoroughly checked the ingredients I put out on the work surface. I sent her to wash her hands and checked that Tom was still sleeping. Unlike Inbal, who let Nofar handle the ingredients and dirty the kitchen as she pleased, I found it hard to keep my cool whenever Nofar spilled anything with her unsteady hands. Nofar resented my intervention. She was a very independent little girl. Once all the ingredients were in the bowl, Nofar began to mix them awkwardly. I was holding her hands and helping her mix, even though it displeased her, when suddenly Tom woke up and started crying.

"Don't move," I commanded. "Mommy will be right back."

I ran into the bedroom. Tom was awake, his diaper soaked and filthy. I cleaned him up and tried to calm him down, but he cried non-stop. He seemed to be ill. Nofar felt she'd been waiting for too long and thought I'd interfered too much in the baking anyway and continued to mix the ingredients without me. When she finished, she picked up the bowl and brought it to the nursery to show me what she'd done.

"I told you not to go on without me!" I shouted as I rocked Tom from side to side, trying to calm him down. She looked down, and I went on, "Why did you bring it in here? You've probably spread it all over the house!" Her bottom lip began to tremble, and I knew she'd be crying in a matter of seconds. Before I knew it, she turned round and suddenly fell over one of the toys strewn on the floor. The bowl and its contents flew through the air and landed on Tom's bouncer. The whole room was covered with a sticky mixture of flour, sugar and eggs.

"Nofar!" I yelled in distress. "Look what you've done! The entire room's covered in it now!"

Nofar fled to the bathroom, covering the hallway from the nursery to the bathroom with footprints smeared with cupcake mix. I heard her crying in the bathroom and decided to let her cry. I didn't want to comfort her at that moment. I was too angry. I wanted someone to comfort me. Tom, spurred on by Nofar's cries and my screams, cried even more feverishly, and I felt that I was a few seconds away from joining him. The bouncer usually helped soothe him when he was overwrought, but now it was completely covered with batter. I put him in his cot. He wouldn't stop crying. I took the bowl with the leftover mixture to the kitchen, and on the way, I heard Nofar sobbing in the bathroom. Her crying confused me. I was sorry I yelled at her like that, but I wanted her to understand that she needed to be more disciplined. I glanced at the clock. It was already six o'clock. Amir should be on his way home, a welcome thought, especially when there was such a mess to deal with.

"Where are you?" I asked him as soon as I heard him on the line.

"Work."

"You haven't left yet?"

"Why would I? It's barely five thirty."

"It's after six."

"It's still early."

"What's early about six?" I screamed. "Get your stuff and come home now!" I ordered.

"I really can't."

"There no such thing as can't... you just don't want to."

"Come on, Rose," he sighed. "You know what it's like here, and I have a huge presentation tomorrow. I was planning to work late tonight."

"So work from home, after you help me here. Nofar made a terrible mess here and Tom's not well... I need you to come home."

"Can't you ask your mother to come help you?"

"No," I snapped. I could ask, but I really didn't want to. I was sick of him constantly suggesting I ask my mother for help.

"Okay," he replied in an impatient voice. "I'll finish what I can here and get home."

"Make it quick."

"I'll try, but it'll take me at least an hour to finish up."

I knew he wasn't going to get home before eight. I sat in the living room. Nofar was still shut in the bathroom, and Tom was screaming in his cot. I looked at my crying baby and began screaming. I screamed for a few seconds, letting out all the anger and pain. When I finished screaming, I started to cry uncontrollably. I sat on the couch, almost paralyzed, and cried. I couldn't move myself. I was angry with myself for getting into this situation, I hated Amir for putting me in this situation and I felt sorry for my two children who were within reach of me, but I couldn't get myself to comfort them.

After a few minutes, which seemed like an eternity, I got up, went to the kitchen, blew my nose and washed my face. I picked up Tom, whose crying fit had made him hiccup. I kissed his bald head and gently wiped his tear drenched face. He began to relax. I went with him to the bathroom. Nofar was sitting in the corner, her eyes swollen with tears. I leaned over and kissed her on the cheek.

"Come on!" I gestured to her and hugged her with my free hand.

"I didn't mean to make a mess," she said, sobbing.

"I know, darling." I kissed her again. "You need to just be a little more careful and to listen to me more."

"Okay," she said softly.

I washed all of us, heated a frozen pizza for Nofar and breastfed Tom. I decided to leave the mess for Amir. I settled Nofar in our bed and waited for Amir in the living room. He arrived a little after eight thirty. He smiled when he saw me sitting comfortably on the couch with little Tom sleeping on me peacefully. He hadn't yet seen the mess in the kitchen and nursery. He came up to me, kissed me on my forehead and gently stroked Tom's head. "I see the storm's passed," he whispered.

I didn't answer. He realized that I was still angry and turned toward the nursery to see Nofar. He liked to look at her when she was asleep. I stood up and followed him. I wanted to see his reaction at the sight of the mess. Immediately after turning on the light, he stepped back in disbelief. He turned and saw me standing behind him. He had a surprised look on his face.

"What is it?" he whispered. "What happened? Where's Nofar?"

"In our bed," I whispered back. I went into the bedroom and put Tom in his crib.

Amir looked at Nofar, a smile on his face. His smile evaporated within seconds when he turned to me and saw my angry look.

I left the room and returned to the living room. Amir came after me.

"What happened?"

"I wanted to make cupcakes with Nofar, then Tom woke up so I went to him. It was hard for her to wait, and she brought the full mixing bowl to me. I was mad at her and she spilled the entire mixture."

"Intentionally?"

"Of course not, but she just doesn't listen."

"So you yelled at her?"

"Yes," I said without blinking. I couldn't understand how he still had the audacity to criticize me when he himself was never home.

"Was that helpful?" he said critically.

"Yes!" I replied defiantly. "It helped me relax."

"I'm glad to hear it," he said, but I knew he was anything but glad.

"I'm glad you came home so quickly."

"I came as fast as I could. You have no idea what I go through every day."

"*You* have no idea what *I* go through every day."

"Actually, I do... you can't miss it with all the hysterical phone calls and texts." He looked around. "Not to mention the crazy mess that I come home to every night!" He pointed to his surroundings.

"When do you think I have time to clean up?" I yelled in a whisper so as not to wake the children. "You know what it's like taking care of two children alone?"

"Your mother and my mother took care of more than two children by themselves and did it without disposable diapers!"

"Then they must have been magicians. Besides, your father and my father didn't get home this late every day. They had a lot more help."

"Asi also works very late and Daria gets along great with her two kids."

"You must be kidding me!" I laughed bitterly. "Daria has a nanny and maid."

"And what about Inbal?" He hit a nerve. I aspired to be like Inbal.

"David and Inbal's house isn't much tidier than ours. The difference is, I'm sure, that David doesn't conjure up cutting remarks from the 1950s about the house not being clean enough. And while we're talking about David, he helps Inbal much more than you help me."

"He's a firefighter. He works shifts… he can be home for days at a time."

"You could do that, too, if you wanted to."

"If I wanted to be unemployed, you mean?"

"You could work at home if you really wanted to."

He didn't really want to. It was clear. How could he concentrate at home with two small children? I didn't want to either. My maternity leave wasn't over yet and already I wanted to return to work. I was sorry I'd asked to extend it for another three months, but now it was too late. I had no childcare for Tom for the next three months, and I was especially fearful of the way I'd be perceived by others. I remembered how Rina gossiped about me when I hadn't put enough current pictures of Nofar in my office. Returning from my maternity leave after only three months would be considered criminally negligent by others.

When Tom was six months old, he went to daycare, and I returned to work. I'd missed work so much that, for all I cared, Gideon could call me a junior bookkeeper and not a chief one as long as I got to go back to my work routine. Although I was drunk with joy, I couldn't ignore the relationship that had been forged between Gideon and my temporary replacement, Erez. In the early days of my return, I didn't pay any attention to it, as I was so busy getting back into my routine and seeing what had changed during my absence.

A week later, I could no longer ignore the warm relationship between the two. Erez would be closeted in Gideon's office for hours and attended meetings inside and outside the office. I was surprised that Gideon was so enthusiastic about Erez. When I reviewed the situation, I was disappointed to see that Erez hadn't completed many of the tasks assigned to him, and had left me a lot of work that was supposed to have been completed during my maternity leave. At first, I was afraid Erez was going to replace me permanently and I'd find myself out of the door once the law allowed it. I discovered that, during my maternity leave, Erez had finished his internship and was now awaiting his graduation to be a full-fledged CPA. I hoped that the fact that he was still employed through the accounting firm, rather than directly through our company, was a good indication that he wasn't going to become a full-fledged employee at Smart Green.

Two weeks later, my hopes were dashed. Erez became a Smart Green employee, but, to my astonishment, he didn't take my position. He became my immediate supervisor. Gideon called me to his office and told me that, during my absence, he'd been deeply impressed by Erez's managerial abilities and decided to appoint him to the position of CFO, a position that was his own until then.

"I've been thinking about it for a long time," he said. "There's too much pressure on me, and I thought hiring a CFO would reduce the stress."

I looked at him in shock. "You didn't think to ask me first?"

"I thought about it, really I did. If you only knew how much you mean to me and to the company, which is exactly why I didn't offer it to you." I looked at him, shocked.

"You do your job beautifully. Erez wasn't as good at it as you." So he knew Erez only did half the work, and yet he still offered him a position senior to mine. "Erez is more of a businessman, like me. He doesn't like dealing with the finance and the figures. He likes going to meetings and doing deals." I remembered Erez telling me that this was exactly what he wanted to do. When he'd told me he wanted to be a CFO, I'd chuckled. I didn't believe that a guy who'd only just got his certificate could be placed in such a senior role, and I certainly hadn't imagined that he'd get it in the company where I worked.

I soon discovered that, in my absence, Erez had obtained credit lines for the company with two more banks and thus reduced costs by about twenty percent. He also brought in three big new customers and signed huge contracts with existing customers. I had to admit to myself that the guy was talented, but the offense of promoting a guy who was younger than me in age and seniority was too big.

CHAPTER 10

My father's brother was an insurance agent, and when one of his customers told him he was looking for an accountant, he called me immediately. He remembered me telling him that I'd be happy to be an accountant instead of a bookkeeper. I didn't think twice.

Although Gideon tried to appease his guilty conscience by increasing my salary slightly without my even asking, he didn't even consider updating my status by amending the definition of my job from bookkeeper to accountant, and I thought that after three years of work (two-and-a-half if you take into account the maternity leave) and after Erez's meteoric promotion above me, it was the least I deserved. Gideon didn't think so.

A week later, I got the job and two weeks later I was the accountant at AA Spices Ltd. Gideon was shocked when I walked in and handed him my letter of resignation. I didn't understand why he was so surprised. Didn't he understand that he'd pushed me out? I was so drunk from the euphoria of resigning from Smart Green and smiling happily into Gideon's stunned face, that I totally ignored the bad stench that accompanied me as I entered my new position.

AA Spices Ltd. was an importer of spices and ingredients for the food industry. Their warehouse smelled so strongly that, in order to enter it, you had to wear a gas mask. The company offices were connected to the warehouses that were packed with hundreds of sacks of spices. The smell was so intense that, during the first week of my work, I couldn't eat much of anything. Every day I got home, threw my clothes into the washing machine and went to scrub myself in the shower.

I soon realized that the stink wasn't just physical. The transition to the spice company was so fast that I ignored all the warning lights that flickered all around me. All I saw was that I'd gotten a job as an accountant and that I'd improved my pay by about fifteen percent. I ignored the fact that the previous accountant had been dismissed in disgrace because he'd fought with the CEO and that the operations manager, who was the CEO's right-hand man and deputy, gave me goose bumps from the first moment I met him at the interview. I had an uneasy feeling about the man, who appeared to derive perverse pleasure from lashing out at his workers. I knew I wouldn't be answering directly to him, and I was hoping that this was just a fleeting feeling, so I chose to ignore my intuition.

Unfortunately, I was wrong.

I found that the operations manager was also a secondary shareholder in the company and spread terror among the workers. Before I even stepped through the door I was on his blacklist because he'd wanted to appoint a distant relative of his, so that he could control the accounts department. The CEO understood his strategy and chose me, both because I wasn't related to any of them and because I accepted a salary that was about forty percent lower than the operations manager's relative requested.

I realized that I'd find myself out of the company within a few months or years and decided to concentrate on work and try to ignore all the fray going on around me. It very quickly became clear that I didn't have a lot of work to do. The work was monotonous and boring, and I often spent long days browsing aimlessly on the Internet. I had nothing to do; the volume of work didn't justify the employment of a full-time accountant. I'd left an exciting and challenging job with a fascinating company for a monotonous and boring role with a rotten one.

Unfortunately, I had no refuge at home. My relationship with Amir was in the worst state we'd experienced since the day we met. The crisis began during my maternity leave with Tom, when I felt I was sinking into a mountain of diapers, pacifiers and laundry that required constant folding. When I returned to work at Smart Green, Amir initially supported me when I whined incessantly about Erez' surprising appointment, but at some point he grew tired of hearing my incessant complaints. I tired him out with the same stories every day. He was obviously pleased when I went to work for the spice company. He thought, as I did at first, that I could now put my bitterness behind me, but the new situation only worsened my mood. I took out all my anger and frustration on him and the children.

I was so absorbed in myself and my troubles that I completely disconnected myself from the environment. I barely spoke or met with my family or friends. I knew that Daria was pregnant again, but due to my self-imposed isolation, it took me by surprise when I heard that Daria had given birth to her third child. Each time she'd talked to me about the pregnancy, I was sure she was only in mid-pregnancy. I was a bit surprised by the fact that Daria decided to have another child. I thought that two was enough for her. I knew Inbal wanted quite a few children, and I was sorry she hadn't gotten pregnant again.

We all met up at the traditional event organized in honor of Daria's new baby and her rapid return to her pre-baby weight. Daria was standing at the entrance to the hall and flashing a plastic smile at her guests, but when I arrived, she attacked me with hugs and kisses.

"I haven't seen you for so long!" she scolded me. She was right. I'd had no desire to meet with anyone for months.

"I'm sorry," I whispered, looking for the new baby.

"Come on," she said, wrapping her arm around my waist. "Asi's somewhere round here with the stroller. I'll introduce you to our sweet Galia."

Daria pulled me into the yard. Asi was standing calmly under a broad mint tree, pushing the stroller back and forth. "Don't think I've forgotten," she said confidentially.

"Forgotten what?"

"It's your birthday," she winked at me. I smiled. I never made a fuss about my birthday. "Don't leave early, because I have a little surprise for you," she said and went to the stroller and picked up a tiny red-cheeked baby.

I wasn't a very motherly person, and I wasn't usually keen on babies, but this was the sweetest baby I'd ever seen. I couldn't resist holding out my hands to her. Daria carefully handed Galia to me, and she leaned into my embrace so very naturally. I stroked her little cheek and held her tiny hand. Automatically, she grabbed my finger. I bent my head and kissed her little hand.

"She's a cutie, isn't she?" Daria was waiting for my approval.

"Oh, yes," I said, unable to turn my gaze away from the baby. She was simply mesmerizing. Asi came up to me and took the baby away from me almost forcefully. "She's calmed down now, so we should take her back in to see the guests," he said.

I sat down next to Inbal and smiled at her. I knew that the event wasn't easy for her. Adi, her younger daughter, was almost three years old now. Inbal was almost a year older than me, so she was almost thirty-three years old. I knew she wanted at least two more children and time was not in her favor.

"How are you?" she asked as she tied a ribbon in Coral's hair and sent her back to the children's entertainer.

"Excellent," I lied. "And you?"

"Okay." She found it harder to lie than I did.

"Where's David?" I looked around as if searching for him.

"He'll be along later. He's finishing a shift."

"Won't he be tired?"

"They didn't have any callouts on this shift, so he mostly slept," she laughed. "Where's Amir?"

"At home with Tom, who has a fever. Nofar looks as if she's starting to develop something too, so she stayed at home as well," I lied again. In fact, Nofar didn't want to come alone with me.

"Oh, God," she said anxiously. "Nothing serious?"

"I don't think so… just a light stomach virus."

"Yeah, Coral had something similar two weeks ago." I smiled at her with a lack of interest. Gossip about children's viruses had never interested me. I looked at the elderly couple who joined our table and remembered the previous party, two and a half years earlier, when I'd met Lior and Aya. Despite Aya's delight at the thought of us spending our maternity leaves together, I'd stayed confined to home for most of my months off. Our relationship had withered until it just ended completely.

"Where are Aya and Lior?" I asked Daria as she passed by.

"You didn't hear?" she said with a bright smile. I knew she didn't like my friendship with Aya, and was delighted to find that the relationship no longer existed. "They went to Harvard just two months ago."

"What did they go there for?"

"Lior was offered a PhD fellowship as a professor."

"Wow," Inbal marveled. "Weren't they the two lawyers who sat with us at your last event?"

"Yes," Daria said proudly, as if she herself had received the prestigious offer. "An amazingly successful couple."

"What will she do there?" I asked.

"I don't know. The truth is, it always seemed to me that, despite all her success, what she wanted most was to be home with the kids, so now it'll work out well for her. She has another child due soon, so everything's worked out well for her."

"She's pregnant again?" I asked incredulously. "She doesn't waste any time!"

"Yes... she got pregnant fairly quickly after the last birth. I couldn't understand why the matter was so pressing."

I looked at Inbal and saw that this conversation was

painful for her. She couldn't get pregnant for a third time. Quite surprisingly, Daria also noticed Inbal's pain and quickly changed the subject.

"How's it going with your new job?" she asked me. "I understand you've moved to a different company, a very big importer. Asi's heard of them."

"Yes," I smiled in exaggerated modesty. "It's a highly stable company." I couldn't find one good word to add. Luckily, another guest grabbed Daria's attention, and I was spared from having to say any more about AA Spices Ltd.

Little Adi went to Inbal and pulled her from her seat. She wanted her to go and watch the clown who was entertaining the children. I looked at Inbal and the girls, and I felt tears welling in my eyes. I suddenly realized that I spent most of my life feeling negative feelings. I was thirty-two that same day. Just sixteen years ago, that car accident had wiped out all of my childhood memories. Everyone had told me that I was a gifted child and was full of life, an excellent student and a good athlete. Out of all of the girls in our high school, David the hunk had chose me to be his girlfriend. Where did that girl disappear to? Did the memory loss make me lose my personality too?

I felt I could no longer control my tears and went outside. I headed for my car. I wanted to sit quietly by myself for a few minutes. Right at the entrance to the parking lot, I almost collided with David, who was just arriving.

"Hey... hey!" He grabbed me by my hand. "What happened?"

I didn't want him to see me crying, and I turned my face away from him. "Nothing," I said.

"It doesn't look like nothing," he said and took out a

small packet of tissues from his pocket and pulled one out. He wiped my cheek gently and handed me the tissue so I could finish the job.

We sat on a small staircase leading to the entrance of an abandoned building.

When my crying had subsided and my breathing was back to its regular rhythm, he asked gently, "Now will you tell me what happened?"

"Nothing, really." He looked at me incredulously. "I mean, nothing specific," I corrected myself. "I just feel like a complete failure."

"You're absolutely not a failure."

"Believe me, I am." I blew my nose again. "I can't do anything right in my life."

"What do you mean? You have a great husband, two beautiful children and a good job."

"Yeah, right," I said in a disgruntled tone.

"What ? You think no one else has problems?" He patted my shoulder. "You think no one else ever has a crisis? Having difficulties and problems in life doesn't make you a failure."

"I don't think you and Inbal have problems and difficulties."

"Sure we do." He looked at me in a familiar way. I recognized it from the hospital, when I was sixteen. "But we overcome them."

I looked at him quizzically. This man could have been my husband. This amazing man, with the beautiful blue gaze, had loved me once. I knew he had loved me, but I couldn't ever remember the feeling. For the first time since the accident, sixteen years earlier, I had the strange feeling that I was beginning to remember the way I'd felt.

We were sitting next to each other, and suddenly I

pressed my lips to his. I have no idea where I got the courage to do that. At first, I felt him respond to my kiss, but suddenly he grabbed me by the shoulders and distanced himself from me forcibly.

"What are you doing?" he said, shocked… or angry. I couldn't quite interpret his response.

I looked down and when I lifted my eyes again, he was walking determinedly toward the hall. He was just across the road, and I wanted to say something… apologize, explain, try to kiss him again… I didn't know what I wanted, but I didn't want him to go further away.

"David!" I shouted. He turned to me. "Wait!" I begged, and I started running toward him.

PART B

CHAPTER 11

I woke up in a hospital. This time, I remembered the accident. I thought the odds were amazing: exactly sixteen years after I turned sixteen, I was injured in a car accident in exactly the same way. Although I didn't remember anything from my first accident, I knew what I'd been told about it. Just like the first time, David was on the other side of the road, and I was running to him when a car hit me.

When I opened my eyes, I didn't know how long I'd laid there in the hospital. Once again, I was surrounded by a whole team of doctors and nurses who looked at me in surprise. From the first moment I opened my eyes, I had a strong and strange feeling of déjà vu. The staff seemed familiar to me.

"How long have I been here?" I asked in confusion.

"Two weeks," replied one of the doctors.

I thought it was more than strange, even funny, that I'd woken up two weeks after the accident, just like last time. I was terrified by the fact that, once again, I'd had an accident, and I was in the hospital - again. Have I forgotten anything? I asked myself and the question itself made it clear to me that, this time, I hadn't suffered memory loss.

A few minutes later, the staff dispersed, and one of the nurses called my parents. I was surprised they hadn't called Amir. I figured that Amir was probably concerned about bringing little Tom to the hospital because he might catch something. My parents approached my bed… and I looked at them in amazement. They looked considerably younger than I remembered. Maybe I was just confused; maybe my vision was blurred.

"Rose," my father whispered. "I'm so glad you woke up."

"We were so worried," my mother said, sobbing.

"I'm fine," I muttered. I couldn't tear my eyes from my parents… They were so young! I studied my mother, who was wearing a dress I hadn't seen in years. "Where's Amir? And the children?" I asked, and my parents looked at me like I'd just arrived from the moon. I couldn't understand why my question seemed so strange to them.

Then my father asked, "Who's Amir?"

I opened my eyes wide in surprise, and Mom started crying.

My father dragged her out to the hallway. I overheard the doctor explaining to them that it made sense that I'd be confused and that it was possible that I'd suffered temporary or permanent memory loss. In the background, I heard Nurit, my younger sister, asking to enter my room. The nurse waved her in and, to my amazement, the sister who entered my room wasn't the twenty-eight-year-old version I remembered, but her twelve-year-old self. I let out a cry and covered my mouth with my hand. Nurit fled, and my mother ran into the room.

"What happened, Rose?"

"Uh... oh... can I..." I stuttered heavily, "Uh... could I... have a mirror?"

My mother stroked me gently. "Rose, you've been through a pretty bad accident... your face is a little swollen. Are you sure you want a mirror?"

"Yes... yes..." I continued to stutter. "I need a mirror."

My mother left the room and returned after five long minutes with a small mirror. She handed it to me... I raised it slowly. I closed my eyes and opened them when I knew that the mirror was right in front of me.

The image reflected back at me was my sixteen-year-old self.

It took me two days to get over the shock. The doctors and my parents thought I was just disoriented from the accident, but this time I wasn't confused at all. I remembered every detail up until the accident. That is, up until the accident I had when I was thirty-two. In my head, the year was 2012, and I was a thirty-two-year-old accountant and a mother of two. But the reality was that it was 1996; physically, I was sixteen and a high school student.

At first I thought I was dreaming, but I didn't seem to wake up from it, and the reality was too tangible. Then, I developed a theory that the years I thought I'd experienced from age sixteen to thirty-two were all just a dream. The problem was that this time around, I still couldn't remember anything that happened to me before the age of sixteen. I knew everyone around me, not because I remembered my childhood memories, but because I remembered all the stories people had told me about my life up to the age of sixteen. That's what I started calling my memories of the last sixteen years, which were seared in my mind - my previous life.

This time, the doctors didn't diagnose amnesia. I remembered all the names of my family and friends, and I had some idea about the events that had taken place prior to the accident, including the accident itself. My knowledge came from the stories that people had told me in my previous life. I didn't actually remember anything that occurred before my sixteenth birthday. It took me a while to understand that the information I had about my life didn't come from my memory, but from stories people had told me. When there was a missing part of a story, my memory couldn't fill in those missing pieces and those around me simply assumed that the accident had caused me some confusion.

Everyone was sure it was a miracle I'd survived the accident. I heard the doctor tell my parents that he was pleased I hadn't suffered a serious head injury in the accident. To him, my brain seemed fine. No severe injury was diagnosed, but I knew that the truth was not as it seemed. I knew I had some problem that conventional medicine couldn't explain: In my mind, I was thirty-two, not sixteen. I also knew I couldn't tell anyone what was happening to me; stories about previous lives would land me straight in a psychiatric unit.

I was lonely. I'd been through a trauma, and there was no one I could share it with. Despite the difficulties I'd experienced with Amir in the weeks before the accident, I missed him. I needed him. I needed to hear him, wanted him to calm me down. In addition, I missed my kids so badly, especially Tom. Now that the children were only a memory from another life, I could admit to myself that he was my favorite child. During the first weeks of my new life, I dreamed of Nofar and Tom almost every night and ended up waking up in tears. I was a mother without children; I had no apparent reason to mourn children who, in my new reality, had never even been born.

About two weeks after I woke up, David came to see me, just like last time.

Because in my previous life, I chose not to continue my relationship with him, I had very few stories to compensate for my erased memory. He sat on my bed and held my hand.

"How are you?" he said, holding back his tears.

I looked at him, transfixed. He was the last person I remembered seeing before the accident, but the memory I had was of the thirty-three-year-old David, not the seventeen-year-old David. I preferred him as an adult. He was a fairly handsome boy, but was much more impressive as a grown man. His body was still adolescent and he had unflattering facial hair adorning his upper lip.

"I'm okay..." I replied. "I mean, so-so... I'm very confused."

"Of course, you've been through a terrible accident," he said, leaning over and kissing my forehead. He smelled strongly of sweat, the sweat of a teenager who was not yet used to using scent and deodorant or shaving his face. I longingly remembered his pleasant smell and the masculine stubble on his face when I'd kissed him only a few weeks earlier.

Suddenly I realized that, dream or no dream, I now had a chance to fix what I'd done wrong in my previous life. Last time, I'd chosen to leave David; this time I could choose to stay with him. Last time, I'd left David

MICHAL HARTSTEIN

because I hadn't known him, but this time I knew him - I knew him as a loving husband, a devoted father and a very sexy man.

This time he'd be *my* man, the father of *my* children.

Nofar and Tom.

Were they a hallucination? Or reality? Their memory was so strong and real. Should I give up a man I knew I desired and was in love with just because of a memory of something I wasn't even sure was real? Should I give up a man - a boy - who was in love with me with every fiber of his being?

David put his head to my head, our eyes met, and I smiled at him. I raised my hand and pressed his mouth to mine. I kissed him and he kissed me back. This time he didn't object. didn't run.

"I don't want to hurt you," he said in a trembling voice.

"It's okay," I smiled. "I won't break."

For David, we simply continued where we had left off. For me, it was, in fact, a completely new relationship. I didn't know David as a partner. I didn't have any memories of us as a couple. While I could bridge the gap between my missing childhood memories with the ones I had in my past life, I had no memories of David. In my previous life, we broke up after the accident and, apart from when I met him as Inbal's husband, I had no shared memories with him. I had to lie a lot. I didn't want to reveal the fact that I mostly didn't remember him. I didn't want to hurt him. When there was no choice, I'd confess that I probably didn't remember because of the accident, and I usually allowed him to rehash shared memories while I nodded in agreement as if I recalled them as well.

Going back to school was difficult. I felt out of place. In my head, I was thirty-two, and returning to my youth wasn't easy. My parents didn't understand why the accident had made me so stubborn and impatient. They said that before the accident I was easy going.

That was because I wasn't just a child.

I woke up as a woman.

Slowly, I began to get used to my situation. I managed to stop seeing everything through the eyes of an adult and went back to enjoying the youth I'd regained. This time, I went back to high school as David's girlfriend, which made my return easier on me. Last time, I'd been confused; this time, I knew exactly what I wanted.

I wanted David.

Whenever David and I could find somewhere to make love, he'd tell me that, while he obviously wasn't happy that I'd had the accident, he had to admit that, now, the sex was absolutely amazing! Theoretically, we were the same age, but in terms of sexual development, we were each at our peak and every encounter between us created sparks.

Reuniting with Daria and Inbal as girls was also strange. I always remembered Daria as a stunning girl. She was, indeed, very beautiful, but my memories had intensified her beauty. Inbal, on the other hand, was engraved in my memory as a plump girl. In reality, she was only a little larger than us. As a grown woman, she was bigger. She seemed far more beautiful than I remembered, and I was afraid that, in this second chance I was enjoying, she'd steal away my David and take my place as his spouse. I observed her many times, watching her intently. Were it not for the memory of my past life, I wouldn't have imagined she was secretly in love with David. She was a loyal friend and knew to keep her distance.

.

CHAPTER 12

If, during the first year of my 'new life,' as I'd nicknamed my life after the second accident, I still thought my 'previous life' was a dream or a hallucination, time showed me that my previous life had been real. I didn't know what kind of reality it was and exactly how I'd changed my life and traveled back in time, but I knew I was reliving my life.

Toward the end of my studies in high school, I relived the death of my grandfather, who had died on exactly the day he'd died in my previous life. I was very close to Grandfather Reuben, my mother's father. He had been a legendary commander in the Independence Day War and most of the stories about him had never been told. Although he was a military man, he was an extremely gentle man and treated his children and grandchildren with dedication and love. This time, because I knew the date of his death, I made sure to spend time with him in his last hours. It was also the only time I nearly told my mother the strange reality of my life. She noticed that I initiated a visit to him the night before he died. She asked me if I knew he was going to die. Her question startled me and for a moment I thought maybe she'd noticed that I often knew what was going to happen, but she actually suspected that my grandfather was very sick and only I knew about his illness. I was glad he was the only relative of mine who had died in my previous life, because knowing when a loved one was going to die and having to wait for it was unbearable. On the day of my grandfather's death, I had no doubt that I was reliving my life. This wasn't a fleeting feeling of déjà vu. I remembered incidents that occurred in my private life, in the country and the world. I had never been a big follower of current events, so I didn't remember most events in Israel or worldwide. I remembered more or less who was prime minister, but I couldn't remember exactly when the elections were held or when we had wars.

Surprisingly, I didn't experience the butterfly effect. I remembered seeing that film starring Ashton Kutcher, which was released only eight years after I awoke. My new life surprisingly resembled my previous life except that, this time, I chose to be with David. Most of the time, I didn't bother comparing the two, but just got on with living my life as if it was the first time. I'd forgotten most of the experiences, so I didn't feel like I was in an eternal rerun.

When Daria invited me to her discharge party, I knew I had to go. I wanted to see Amir again. I remembered how, in my previous life, Asi was actually more interested in me, which increased Daria's interest in him. This time, I went with David. We met Inbal at the entrance to the club, and we all went in together.

Once again, Daria was going around the club surrounded by friends and admirers. She was wearing the same bright mini-dress that I remembered. We went over. She was talking with Amir and Asi. I knew their names despite the fact I'd never met them in my new life.

"Inbal! Rose! David!" She jumped on us. "I'm so glad you came."

"As if we could have missed this party!" I smiled warmly.

"Inbal said she wasn't sure she'd come." Daria looked at Inbal accusingly.

"I was supposed to stay on the base for the entire weekend," Inbal tried to defend herself.

"What's important is that all of us are here," I said, and the three of us had a group hug.

"Meet," Daria introduced the two men who stood beside her as we approached, " Amir." She pointed to my previous husband. "And... " She tried to remember.

"Asi," I whispered in my heart.

"Asi," Asi put in and reached out his hand to shake ours.

This time Asi didn't blush in embarrassment. He immediately understood I was with David and showed no interest in me.

I found it hard not to stare at Amir. I knew him better than anyone else in the world. I'd lived half of my life and almost all of my previous life with him. My heart ached. He was so strong and handsome, and I remembered that he'd neglect himself over time and would end up gaining weight. Even though we'd had difficult times, I missed him. He was the closest thing to home I'd ever had.

"Amir," she tapped lightly on Amir's shoulder, "is our

new operations officer, and Asi is his friend from basic training."

"Where are you based?" Asi took an interest.

"I'm in Zrifin, David's in Central Command and Inbal's in Tel Hashomer," I answered for the three of us.

"Nice." He smiled.

His smile was devoid of any interest in me, and I wondered if, this time, Daria would make him a target. I soon realized that her goal this time was completely different.

"What do you think about Amir?" she asked me when we both excused ourselves to go to the bathroom.

"Amir?" I opened my eyes. Never in a million years would I have thought that Daria would be interested in Amir.

"Come on... the cool officer I introduced you to earlier."

"Yes," I pretended to remember. "Amir..."

"Did you look at him? What do think?" she asked briskly as she fixed the makeup under her eyes.

"I didn't really notice him that much," I lied. From the moment we entered, I used every opportunity I got, when no one was paying attention, to stare at Amir. This situation, where I could watch Amir as a young man again, appealed to me. "I haven't got much to say about him," I lied again, because, honestly, I could tell her how he liked his coffee in the morning and that his most obnoxious habit was sitting and picking his belly button. I knew what excited him, what made him laugh, what he liked to eat, and where he'd rather go on vacation. "Why do you ask?"

"I've got a small crush on him." She smiled a crooked smile, and I felt all the blood in me rush straight to my feet.

"Is he really your type, anyway?"

"I've decided I don't have a type," she laughed, pleased at her own joke. "He's just cute and has a good head on his shoulders. He also gives the impression of being a very sensitive guy."

Daria was exactly right. Amir was all the things she'd said. I didn't fall in love with him in my previous life for no reason.

"He only came to us recently... it's too bad it only happened now that I'm being released."

For a moment I relaxed; perhaps nothing would come of this crush.

"But I'm not about to give up such a catch just because I'm not a soldier anymore!"

I wanted to see Amir again, but only as a one-time thing. I hoped that what was the beginning of the most significant relationship in my previous life would be nothing more than a fleeting acquaintance in my new life.

A week later, we - Amir, Asi, Daria and I - were once again sitting in the little café where we'd met in my former life, and where Amir and I started our relationship. This time, there were six of us since David came with me, and Daria made sure Inbal came so that Asi wouldn't feel alone. Daria continued her efforts to conquer one of the guys, only this time she had her sights set on Amir.

"Where do you girls know each other from?" Amir asked in interest.

"We've been friends since kindergarten," Daria replied immediately.

"Oh, wow..." He was impressed. "Well done. I was in the United States with my parents and only came back when I was in second grade, and later on we moved around, so I've no friends from way back."

"Wow, lucky you," I said, just as I did last time.

"That I moved?"

"No," I laughed. "That you got to grow up in a different country."

"I don't remember a thing."

"Why?" Inbal asked with interest. I already knew the answer.

"I don't know… I have fragments of memories of our stay in the United States. We were there for a total of three years, and I was very young. Do you remember yourself in kindergarten?"

"We do." Daria pointed at Inbal and herself. "But she ," Daria pointed at me and smiled, " she doesn't remember a lot of things."

"What does that mean?"

"I had an accident when I was sixteen, and some of the things that happened to me before the accident were erased from my memory," I explained to him again, only this time I was lying when I said that my memory was only partially lost.

"You're not serious," he said in a manner implying it was both a statement and a question.

"No. Really…" This time I was less embarrassed than the last time. To me, it felt as if he'd already heard this story.

"Wow." His eyes opened wide once again. "This is the first time I've ever heard of someone who's forgotten their past."

I smiled.

"Did you have to learn to read and write again at sixteen?" he continued.

"No, my semantic memory wasn't damaged."

"What does that mean?"

"It means I remembered how to speak, write and read, even in foreign languages. I remembered how to solve mathematical equations and all sorts of historical facts."

"Did you remember your friends?"

"Yes. I mean, not everything, but most things I remember," I lied. I couldn't remember a thing.

"Well, we didn't become friends for no reason," Daria answered for me. She didn't like that attention had been focused on me and changed the topic of conversation to her favorite subject : herself.

Two days earlier, she'd enrolled in beauty school. She told us about an unpleasant incident: one apprentice dyed another apprentice's hair a shocking pink. Daria told the story and couldn't stop laughing. We mainly sat around her and smiled embarrassed smiles; we didn't really get the joke.

"You had to be there to really understand how funny it was," she giggled when she realized she was the only one laughing.

"What are you going to study?" Amir asked Inbal, David and me.

"They have some time left to serve," Daria replied immediately, fearing that the conversation would again focus on others. "They won't be released from the army until after the academic year begins, so they won't begin going to university this year."

"Bummer," Amir said. "I'm not going to be released for at least another eight months, so it won't affect my school year in any case."

"You know what you want to study?" David was interested.

"Amir is a computer genius," Daria immediately interrupted and bragged.

"I'm not a genius," he smiled modestly. "Just interested in it. I'll probably go in for software engineering."

"Rose is also a computer genius." David showed off and I looked at him in surprise. Where did he get that from? "At the beginning of the year, when everyone was scared about the millennium bug," David went on, "she was the only person I knew who kept saying nothing would happen." Obviously I knew - it was the second time I'd ushered in the new millennium.

"So you also plan on doing something with computers?" Amir asked.

"I'm really not a computer genius," I corrected the wrong impression that David had given. "And, no, I'm not going to go into that field." I smiled.

"Rose is going to be a lawyer," Daria said knowingly. "If you get into any trouble, you'll know where to turn." She winked. The previous disappointments in my past life had led me to change my career path and study both law and accountaning, just as Lior and Aya had, rather than economics and accounting as I had the first time around.

After a few months, I had to just accept that Daria and Amir's relationship was a sealed deal. I had to repeatedly meet my husband from my previous life, pretend every time that he was a stranger to me and that it was the first time I was hearing all of his stories. What was equally surprising, though not as interesting to me, was the fact that Inbal and Asi struck up a relationship, too. In my previous life, I'd never have imagined Inbal and Asi becoming a couple. I'd fantasized often about David as a partner and had a feeling that Amir had, maybe, harbored a little crush on Daria, which was probably the reason that Daria's relationship with Amir was intolerable to me, but Asi and Inbal getting together was a really strange surprise. He came across to me as a suave, materialistic guy,while she was always humble and spiritual. I soon discovered that, at least in Asi's case, his choice of partner made a dramatic change in his life.

Four years of my new life passed, and I thought less and less of my strange situation. I was just living my life. The fact that we got settled again in pairs with the same three guys, just in a different order, fascinated me. I thought that was probably the universe's way of maintaining balance.

David and I were released from the army almost at the same time and planned our after-army trip. David wanted to go to India, and I wanted to go to the United States. In my previous life, David went to India with Inbal and that's where their love story began. I was supposed to go with Inbal and just gave it up. I ended up going to France for a short trip. I decided that, this time, I wouldn't give up, because we were released at the end of 2000 and planned to travel in the spring of 2001. In September 2001, I knew that New York would change forever and never go back to being the same New York. I thought a lot about the 9/11 attacks. There were very few historical events that I remembered from my past life, let alone their exact date, but September 11th was a universal concept. I considered contacting the security forces or the secret services, but I knew there was nothing I could say that wouldn't make me sound completely crazy or utterly suspicious, especially since I knew my prophecies would come true. David found it difficult to give up on his trip to India, but after I planned a trip which included a whole month trekking in the Rocky Mountains and Yosemite Park, he was convinced.

We traveled for four months. In my previous life with Amir, we went to the United States for a much shorter trip in the spring of 2010. We left Nofar with my parents, so we had to settle for a short, two-week trip that only took in New York, Washington DC and Niagara Falls. I remembered my trip with Amir, and I was surprised at how easy it was to travel to the United States before 9/11. When I went with Amir in 2010, we spent half a day at the US embassy getting a visa. This time, the travel agency just sent our passport to the embassy and we got our visa. When David and I landed at JFK, I was surprised at the sparse security forces and inspection facilities compared to what I remembered from my 2010 visit with Amir. In the spring of 2001, reality was completely different. David didn't understand why I insisted on visiting the Twin Towers and going all the way to the top. To him, they were two skyscrapers just like dozens of others, not very tall, not very old, and not very interesting architecturally. He didn't understand why I insisted on standing in line on the ground floor to reach the observation deck.

Half a year later, as we sat, stunned, in front of the TV, he didn't stop reminding me how lucky we'd been to have gone there when we'd had the opportunity. I looked at the TV screen, my eyes were flooded with tears. The first time I witnessed the disaster, I'd sat, simply stunned. This time I cried... I felt guilty. I kept thinking that maybe I could have prevented the disaster, but I hadn't. I knew I couldn't do anything. Reality was somewhat more complex than my little world. I couldn't fix the world all by myself. Dozens of attacks and disasters occurred during my former life, but I just couldn't remember their dates. The minute Google became available, I could research past events, but not future ones. The fact that Inbal, Daria and I hooked up with the same three guys proved to me that it was impossible to change the future substantially, but I decided that, since I had the opportunity to relive my life, I wouldn't waste it. I'd try not to make the same mistakes I'd made in my previous life.

CHAPTER 13

Once again, Daria got married first. I couldn't remember the exact date she married Asi in my previous life, but I remembered that it was in the spring of 2003. Once again, she stood under a canopy in April 2003, but this time she was standing next to Amir, my previous husband. In my previous life, Amir was the one that was anxious to get married. His parents were traditional people, and it had bothered them that he was living in sin with me. This time, he had no trouble convincing the bride to settle down. Daria was glad of any opportunity that allowed her to be the center of attention. In the past, I had downplayed the modest diamond ring Amir had given me. Unlike me, Daria made sure that everyone admired the impressive diamond ring Amir gave her. Although I wasn't a fan of diamonds and jewelry, I couldn't help but be secretly angry at Amir for investing much less in me and our previous existence together.

A year later, exactly one week before the original wedding date Amir and I had chosen, Inbal and Asi also got married. I couldn't help but love this couple. Asi, in my previous life, had always looked nervous and obsessed with pleasing Daria and her endless whining and requests. Inbal was a much more relaxed and pleasant woman than Daria and, with her, he blossomed. When he was with Daria, Asi could barely squeeze a sentence in, and if he did, then he was interrupted because Daria always made a point of finishing his sentences and speaking for him. Now that Asi was married to Inbal, I got to know him a little better and found out that, apart from being a great trader, he was, just like Inbal, a bookworm and loved to travel. With Daria, he only went on short trips to various European capitals, with the main goal of shopping. With Inbal, he traveled to exotic and fascinating places.

When Inbal was with David, the two of them had lived on the salary of a teacher and a firefighter and had to settle for simple vacations in the country. With Asi, she could afford to travel to places she could only have dreamed about in my previous life. Although Daria was a very impressive woman, especially compared to Inbal, who was always a little chubby and never bothered to pamper herself, Asi had never seemed as in love with Daria as he was now, but with Inbal. Due to the time that had passed, his image in my memory from my previous life was a little vague, but my feeling was that he'd become a more handsome man.

I waited impatiently for Inbal and Asi's wedding. I remembered Inbal's exciting wedding to David, which had overwhelmed me with feelings of negative jealousy. I wondered if she would get married at the same intimate café. I knew that she had planned her wedding with David and assumed she'd probably plan this wedding too. When I received the wedding invitation, it became clear to me that this wedding wouldn't be a repeat of the other exciting occasion. Asi had a huge family and, this time, the bride didn't have a limited budget. Although Inbal's wedding to Asi wasn't as ostentatious and extravagant as Asi's previous wedding had been, this time it was a prestigious garden event, not in a tiny café.

I decided to keep the café for my wedding to David. I wanted to recreate the exciting wedding David and Inbal had enjoyed, with me as the excited bride to be this time around. To be honest, it wasn't that important for me to get married. Neither David nor I came from religious homes, and a religious ceremony meant nothing to us. But I wanted to get married in an exciting and intimate ceremony, like Inbal had, back then. Although it was hard to watch Amir fall in love and marry Daria, I didn't regret the choice I made in my new life. David was a loving and romantic partner, and the sexual chemistry between the two of us was unending, even after years together. I knew that, this time, I'd be extra cautious and not get pregnant as soon as I did with Nofar. I decided that, this time, I wouldn't have any regrets about my professional life.

"Would you like to get married?" David asked me in an amused voice as we left Inbal and Asi's wedding.

"You know the answer... not yet."

"I'm just checking," he explained. "We received so many good wishes in the past three hours, I thought you might change your mind."

"I do want us to have a little ceremony," (I knew exactly what kind of ceremony), "but only in a year, when I finish my studies."

"I don't think I'll finish my studies in another year," he said. David began working as a firefighter after his military service as a temporary job to support us and his geology studies. I knew from my past life that, in the end, he wouldn't make use of his degree, and would become a permanent firefighter.

"Like if you were studying, you'd lift a finger and help me plan the wedding," I laughed. "The bride's always the one who plans everything… you'll just turn up like one of the guests."

"I'll try not to be late," he laughed and I joined him.

We got married a year later, six months later than David's original wedding to Inbal. The café I so wanted to get married in closed down two months before we got married. The building was to be demolished, and in its place they were going to build a luxury apartment hotel. I remembered that the place had been shut down, but I didn't remember that it was right then. I wished I hadn't postponed the wedding. I didn't have time to look elsewhere for a place with a similar atmosphere. Everything in my head was in accordance with David and Inbal's previous wedding, and once I realized that I couldn't replicate the experience that I'd fantasized about, marriage no longer interested me. If it were up to me, we could have canceled the wedding or gotten married in a civil ceremony, but my mother wouldn't hear of it. She was happy that my delusional idea of a wedding in a café had fallen through and arranged a wedding that, unsurprisingly, resembled my first wedding to Amir.

My first disappointment from David came without him even realizing what he did wrong, or rather what he hadn't done. It was a hundred days after we got married. I was hoping that David would celebrate our first hundred days as a married couple with me, just as he had with Inbal.

One hundred days just after we were married, I was

all prepared for the surprise awaiting me. I was careful not to make any appointments for that day, and I managed to avoid tiring duties in court. I wanted to leave early and be fresh and alert for the 'surprise' David was supposed to set up for me. I came home relatively early, showered and prepared clothes for the 'spontaneous' outing I was expecting. By nine o'clock, I really was surprised - David didn't even come home.

"Where are you?" I asked in an angry voice.

"What do you mean, where am I?" he replied, shocked. "I'm at the station. I'm on shift now. I was sure you knew." To be honest, I hadn't bothered to check his shift pattern. I was just confident that, for our hundredth day, he'd organize a romantic surprise for me.

"I was sure you wanted to do something…"

"What?" he asked aloud in a curious voice.

"I don't know… go out and celebrate."

"Celebrate what?"

"We've been married now for exactly one hundred days."

"Really?" he asked and his question stabbed me right in the heart.

"Yes, really," I replied angrily. He didn't understand why I was angry. We hadn't made plans, but I couldn't help thinking that I wasn't getting enough attention. Amir had bought Daria an engagement ring that was much bigger and more impressive than the one he'd gotten me, and David had remembered to surprise Inbal when they celebrated their first hundred days as a married couple, which, of course, I couldn't tell him. Why didn't I get that sort of attention? Why was I not able to awaken such romantic feelings in either of these two men?

I was angry and I was frustrated, but I decided I

wouldn't become such a bitter woman in my new life or, at least, I'd try not to be. I started my internship with a prestigious law firm and decided that, in my new life, I would achieve everything I hadn't in my previous life. This time, I didn't get pregnant unexpectedly. This time, I went to school and chose the right major for me - law and accounting. So what if we didn't celebrate our hundredth day anniversary? I still had a whole life to relive again, and I was going to make the best of it.

I tried to get accepted as an intern with the firm where Aya had interned, but they wouldn't take interns who had graduated in my semester. I sometimes got to see Aya and Lior in the faculty. It was strange to see them as young adults. I decided not to approach them. I didn't want to change the way of the world. We weren't supposed to know each other yet. Occasionally, I encountered them and once I borrowed Aya's summaries of corporate law, but beyond that I treated them like the rest of the students, although I knew them well, mainly due to the fact that their future lay before me like an open book. My future, however, was an enigma to me. I had changed the course of my life and that led to a change in the life-course of everyone around me.

CHAPTER 14

A year after we failed to celebrate our first one hundred days of marriage, my parents, David and I went to Jerusalem to get my license to practice as a lawyer, six months earlier than I had received my accountant's license in my previous life.Studying law takes six months more than accounting, but accounting has a year-longer internship. I worried for the entire ride. I remembered that, in my previous life, I'd figured out I was pregnant with Nofar on the ride to my graduation. My period was a few days late, and I began to fear that history would repeat itself. I remembered that in the pregnancies I'd experienced in my previous life, one of the first symptoms I'd noticed, besides the nausea, was my enlarged breasts. I had no nausea, so I decided to feel my chest and check if there was any change.

"What are you doing?" David whispered with a smile. "Your parents are in the front seat." He thought I was trying to seduce him.

"Nothing," I said. "Someone at work found a lump in

her breast, so I'm worried."

"What lump?" My mother turned around in panic.

"Nothing, nothing."

"What's nothing?" My mother wouldn't calm down. "Who has a lump in her breast?"

"You don't know her."

"We're lucky Rose didn't study medicine," David chuckled. "She'd probably think she's sick with every disease she's studied!"

"It's not funny." My mom wiped the smile off his face. "Breast cancer's no joke, but don't you worry," she looked at me reassuringly, "you're still very young and we've no family history of the disease."

I smiled and she returned to sitting upright in her seat facing the road. Breast cancer didn't bother me at all. I knew with complete certainty that I didn't have breast cancer and that I'd be quite safe from it at least until the age of thirty-two. I was afraid that I was pregnant.

I asked to stop on the way, and I went to the same Super-Pharm store where my mother had bought me a pregnancy test almost sixteen years earlier. I said my head hurt and I wanted to buy some Advil. This time, my mother didn't come in with me; she didn't suspect a thing. I went to the same cubicle and did the test.

Only one bar appeared on the stick.

It didn't calm me down because I knew that in the early days of pregnancy, the hormones aren't strong enough and sometimes you don't see a positive result on the first try with a home test. Two days later, I woke up and discovered to my delight that I wasn't pregnant. I'd probably just been nervous about the ceremony and because the partner at the firm I worked for told me that they couldn't hire me after my internship period. He was nice enough to allow me to work in the office an additional month after the end of my internship, so I'd be able to find an alternative job. When I worked at the accounting firm, it was understood that after the internship was over, interns stayed on as a permanent employee. There was no justice: the story here was different, and I wasn't ready for it. After a year of being used as an errand girl and being sent on a variety of boring missions, I thought that getting my license would allow me to be assigned to more challenging cases so I could really find my niche in the office. However, they had no need of another lawyer in the office, and I didn't want to continue to do the work of an intern. That wasn't why I'd changed my profession.

Two months later, I was sitting in my new office in a new fancy office building. The fact that I had a double degree in law and accounting helped me get into Cohen, Lifshitz & Co., one of the leading law firms in the commercial sector in Israel. One of the partners in the tax department had been my professor on the accounting faculty, and he had recommended me. I was now in his department, which was the most prestigious and central department in the office. I was happy. I felt that the experience I'd gained in my previous life had finally come in handy. I couldn't remember the exact amount I'd earned with the accounting firm where I'd worked at this exact time in my previous life, but I had no doubt my salary as a junior lawyer was significantly higher than my salary as a junior accountant. At first, I thought I got a salary that was especially high due to the fact that I had been on the Dean's List and because of my double degree but I soon discovered that, in the prestigious tax department, there were people who had excelled more than I had and had more impressive diplomas. My starting salary was standard for a junior lawyer.

About three months after I started working at Lifschitz, Cohen & Co., I was still in my office. It was already six in the evening, but I had no intention of calling it a day yet. I was absorbed in reading the reports and analyzing the income tax affidavits of a company whose tax plans were on the verge of being canceled by the tax authorities.

The phone rang. "Rose!" Sarah, the secretary with the squeaky voice squeaked out my name.

"Yes?" I asked impatiently.

"Where are you?"

"What do you mean?" I panicked. I was afraid that someone thought I'd left for home before six. "I'm here at the office."

"No," she laughed, "I know you're in the office. I saw you before." I was surprised because she usually left at five. "Why aren't you in the conference room?"

"There's a meeting?" I panicked again.

"Your head's in the clouds!" She roared with squeaky laughter. "There's the Chanukah candle lighting in the conference room. Come on. Everyone's waiting for you!"

I marked my place in the document and ran to the conference room. The second I entered, I saw Lior standing next to Jacob, the senior partner. I gaped at him in amazement. What was he doing here?

"Ah!" Jacob said in a slightly reproachful tone. "Now that everyone's here, we can get started, but before we begin, I'd like to welcome Lior Steinfeld back from the United States!" He tapped on Lior's shoulder. "To our great satisfaction, Lior's chosen to return to the Holy Land and not settle in a foreign one. I'm sure he can help us all with the knowledge he acquired in studying for his master's degree and the connections he made in New York."

Everyone applauded and welcomed Lior until Jacob silenced them all and asked one of the staff to light the Chanukkia and say the blessing on the candles. After the Chanukkia was lit and we all finished singing Chanukah songs with our out-of-pitch voices, I approached the fancy buffet that was laid out for us, filled my plate with good food and planned to return to my desk to spend the rest of the evening there.

"Rose!" Saul, my former professor, who had recommended me for the job here, startled me when he called my name. My plate jerked in my hand, and I watched the variety of appetizers I had selected so carefully scatter all over the floor. I turned to him with an embarrassed look.

"Oops, sorry," he said in a fatherly tone and signaled the cleaner over to come and pick up the mess. "I want to introduce you to Lior."

"Hello," I said without interest.

"Do you know each other?" Saul was interested and immediately grabbed his forehead. "Of course you do!" he said. "You were both my students."

"True." I smiled.

Lior smiled back. "You do look a little familiar."

"I remember you... your wife also studied at the faculty."

"You know Aya?"

"No." I panicked ! I was talking too much. "I remember you always hung around with someone who also studied at the faculty."

"Yes, I met my wife in college, but how did you know she was my wife? We got married after college."

"I just assumed..." My heart was racing. I knew I could never reveal the real reason I knew him and that all the knowledge I had of him was simply inexplicable. "You were always together, so I assumed you were married."

"Yes," he shrugged and smiled, "well, we are now."

"I understand that you've just returned from the United States."

"Yup."

"What did you do there?" I asked, even though I knew exactly what they'd done in the United States in the past year.

"We both got our MBAs in business management."

"Sounds interesting."

"Yeah, it was really fascinating. Highly recommended."

To be honest, I'd already researched the possibility of going abroad and getting my master's degree, but I found that I couldn't afford such a trip. Unlike Aya and Lior, who could travel together, David would never have joined me, so I put the idea to rest.

"My husband's a fireman," I informed him. The last time we spoke of my husband, he'd been a software engineer. "He doesn't have much reason for taking that long a time abroad."

Lior nodded understandingly. "How long have you been working here?"

"I started in October."

"Nice." He kept nodding. The conversation was stuck. I knew that Lior wasn't good with small talk, and I was afraid to speak. I was afraid that, once again, I'd blurt out information that would reveal the fact that I knew him much better than I was supposed to.

Lior returned to work, and I soon realized why it was

important to Jacob to give him such a warm welcome, and how he'd gained the prosperity that I remembered he and Aya enjoying. Lior was one of the brightest guys I'd ever known. In the world of law, lawyers can be divided into two groups: attorneys in the first group are walking-talking encyclopedias, the kind of people who remember sections of the law and legal matters from the early years of the country; the second group includes the lawyers who barely remember the ground rules, but they always find a way to cut corners and bend the law to suit their clients' requirements. In most offices, there were lawyers of both categories, and they helped each other. Lior belonged to both categories, which was why he was so respected by the other partners and clients. He knew the Income Tax Ordinance almost by heart. He knew the tax regulations fluently, and, in addition, he amazed his clients again and again with his tax planning, which saved them millions of dollars. Jacob wasn't bragging about Lior's return to Israel for nothing. The rumor about Lior being headhunted by one of the major offices in New York had spread quickly, but he'd turned that offer down and returned to Israel for Zionistic reasons, a fact that only intensified people's tremendous admiration for him.

It soon became clear that I myself belonged to the first group. I gained a lot of knowledge, and I liked to flaunt it when I could, but I found it hard to shine with bright new ideas. I didn't have the legal creativity that more senior lawyers in the company had. I found out quickly that, if you didn't have both talents, as Lior did, or at least the ability to creatively bend laws and agreements according to the customer's specification, then your chances of advancing further in the firm or in the business world were limited. It was very difficult for me to accept. In fact, I wouldn't accept the fact that, if you weren't conniving, you wouldn't make it far in the field. I loved the world of law. It was orderly and logical. The accountant in me hadn't disappeared completely and was probably ingrained in me. I went 'by the book' and was angry when my work wasn't sufficiently appreciated.

Lior, essentially, only had one year's experience more than I did. He finished his degree two years ahead of me, but had spent over a year in New York. Nevertheless, his status in the company was that of a lawyer with at least ten years' experience, and I figured his salary suited that status. I tried not to compare myself to him; we were different people, but the comparison I made between myself and the other lawyers was hard on me. I was happy that at least I didn't know everyone's salary. I remembered how knowing about everyone's salaries had made life difficult for me in the past. Many lawyers around were trying to make comparisons and find out how much the others were getting paid, but I preferred not to know. My source of comparison wasn't my salary, but the clients I signed. I kept comparing my clients and clients of other attorneys. I always had a feeling that I was getting the less interesting and less challenging cases. Once they discovered my skills in the field of report reading, they buried me under piles of paperwork. I hardly ever went to meetings or met with clients. I was the brains of the operation, sitting in the office and learning the material so that others could rest on their laurels. Even Lior benefitted from my knowledge, which helped him move forward and succeed. Six months after he returned to Israel and the firm, he began working on a complex portfolio that included the restructuring and transference of assets between companies. I joined him as a junior lawyer, which seemed a bit strange to me due to the fact that the gap between us in terms of seniority wasn't very substantial. I thought they could pair him with an intern and let me lead another case, but this time my fine reputation with financial reports was what set me back.

We sat for weeks and weeks, reading the material. Lior complimented me on my knowledge and diligence, and I had to admit that he was absolutely brilliant. He never stopped coming up with new ideas and finding loopholes in the law that would suit the clients. Because he was responsible for three cases, I was the one who did most of the work. I loved working with him. I learned a lot, but in my heart, I couldn't help but feel that I was doing most of the work and he was getting the credit. On one of the few occasions I went to a meeting with the client, the client gushed with admiration over the ideas we put forward.

"I told you," Jacob told the customer, "you have our most lethal lawyer on your case." He was referring to Lior.

Lior looked at me sheepishly and immediately said, "It's really not just me. It was teamwork." He smiled at me. "Rose Evrony did incredible work here."

"Of course, yes," Jacob said. "Rose has a degree in accounting too. You have a winning team here."

Although I'd also received a compliment, I didn't know how I was showcased when I wasn't there. If not for Lior's comment, Jacob wouldn't have even bothered to bring up my name.

Almost a year after I started working at Cohen, Lifshitz and Co., Saul summoned me to his office and told me that, in honor of the Jewish New Year, I was going to get a slight raise. He explained that, usually, talks about salaries were held in December, but they decided to give me the raise earlier because of the remarkable work I'd done on the case with Lior. I was happy, but not for long. At the toast they made for the Jewish New Year, I realized that the slight salary bump I got was nothing compared to the raise Lior got. Jacob also announced that Lior was about to become the youngest partner in the firm's history. Later, putting together all of the office gossip, I slowly realized that Jacob was mainly concerned that Lior might leave to go to a different firm that was trying to attract him, and so he'd promoted him to the position of partner.

I'd done most of the work and was silenced with a meager wage bump while Lior received the prestigious status of a partner, a corner office with a sea view and a salary I could only dream of. I wondered if, in our previous lives, Lior had become a partner so quickly. Who had helped him with the case last time around? In my previous life, I had only met Lior three years after that case, and he was a partner by then, although he might have been appointed later in his previous life... so, maybe I had accelerated his promotion?

CHAPTER 15

I was so busy working that I was almost completely disengaged from my personal life. Since David was a firefighter and worked shifts, I could afford to work long hours without significantly hurting our relationship. David was actually the only person outside of work I was in touch with. One Friday night, when we arrived for dinner at my mother's, she complained that I didn't bother calling her like my sisters did.

"You only call when you need something," she said.

"But I hardly need anything," I said defensively.

"So you don't call at all!" she said sadly.

My friends got the same treatment, or rather the same non-treatment. Since starting work at Cohen, Lifshitz and Co., I'd spoken with each of them maybe twice. I knew Daria was pregnant, and was especially glad to hear that, this time, Inbal had gotten pregnant faster than in her previous life, only five months after Daria.

I wasn't as involved in the details of Daria's and Inbal's pregnancies as I was last time. In my previous life, I was pregnant myself at that age, so the stories about the nausea, the heartburn, and other uncomfortable things interested me. This time, I was too preoccupied with my career. David asked when we'd try too. I had no answer. The more I thought about it, the more I realized that I didn't know if I even wanted to become a mother. I had been a mother. I hadn't enjoyed it. This time, I felt that my life was going in a more positive direction. Although I wasn't a mastermind in law, my career had progressed in a satisfactory fashion. My salary was already higher than at Smart Green, where, in my previous life, I'd started working only a year-and-a-half later. I didn't have the money issues that I had then, and my marriage was more stable. It was much easier to be a couple with no child to get in the way. I considered not having any children. I didn't understand why everyone had to have a child. When I dared raise the subject with David, he immediately dismissed the idea and said I just wasn't ready yet. He, too, was still enjoying life without children, but he knew he wanted to be a father at some point. I wasn't sure at all that I wanted to be a mother, especially because I'd been one in the past.

When Inbal texted me that Daria had given birth to a girl, I was very happy for her. I was also happy for Inbal, because I knew she wouldn't be saddened at the sight of this baby. She was already four months pregnant this time around. I remembered my Nofar. Despite my difficulties with motherhood, I was suddenly washed with a wave of longing for my lost child. I thought the timing of Daria's pregnancy was amazing. In contrast, there was no doubt in my mind that Inbal's current pregnancy wasn't due to social pressure; I knew she'd been trying for a baby for a long time before Daria, and also before I'd tried (the last time around) and I assumed this time was no different. The fact that Daria was the first to fall for a baby surprised me. Perhaps her pregnancy was unplanned. That thought dazed me. I looked at the calendar and was shocked to discover that it was Nofar's birthday... it was exactly the date of Nofar's birth in my previous life. I knew I had to see the new baby... Nofar's replacement. I hadn't planned on visiting Daria at the hospital - our relationship wasn't as strong as it once was - but I wanted to see her daughter.

I arranged to visit with Inbal, so the visit wouldn't seem unusual, and the two of us drove to the hospital. Daria was lying in bed when we entered the room. She'd combed her hair and put on makeup before our arrival, but we could tell she wasn't doing so great.

"Inbal! Rose!" she exclaimed in fake happiness when we entered the room and went to hug and kiss her. "Forgive me for not getting up," she apologized. "I just can't move... It was a very difficult birth."

Just as it was with my Nofar, I thought.

"Where's the baby?" Inbal was looking around the room for Daria's little daughter.

"She's in the nursery," Daria explained. "They'll bring her in soon so I can try and feed her again."

"You haven't breastfed her yet?" Inbal sounded disappointed.

"Of course I have," Daria replied in an insulted tone. "I mean, I tried, but I haven't succeeded yet." My Nofar had refused to nurse from me.

"Don't worry," Inbal said in a motherly voice, "it'll work itself out."

Or not, I thought. Nofar wouldn't nurse from me at all.

"It's a shame you came," Daria said, and Inbal looked

at her in shock. "I mean, I'm really happy you're here," Daria immediately corrected herself, "but it would have been even better to meet you at the party in honor of the birth." I knew that, without Asi's deep pockets, Daria's parties wouldn't be quite as luxurious as they had been in my previous life.

"We'll come to the party as well," Inbal laughed. "But we couldn't resist coming now, especially Rose." She ratted me out.

"Rose?" Daria looked at me, stunned. "I thought you weren't interested in children."

"I'm interested in you," I lied. I was eager to see the baby.

A few minutes later, Amir rolled the transparent hospital infant crib with the baby in it into the room.

"You're just in time," Daria said. "Look who's here."

"Oh, hello, girls," he smiled. "Rose, I think it must be... well, I haven't seen you for a year now."

Even more, I thought. One of the reasons I chose to break away from the pack was my difficulty with seeing Amir at social gatherings. There was a limit to my acting talent; I found it hard to treat Amir like an acquaintance.

"Busy," I smiled at him.

"How is she?" Daria inquired about her daughter. "Calm?"

"Not very," Amir said, lifting the baby. "But they were able to give her some formula in the nursery."

"Bring her here. Let's see if she's ready to nurse," Daria said, holding out her hands to Amir and the baby.

"Wait up," Inbal jumped in, holding out her hands. "Let's just take a little peep at her... you said yourself she's been fed in the nursery."

Daria nodded to Amir that he could hand the baby to Inbal. "You're not afraid to hold her? I'm scared to death."

"No, I have lots of tiny little nephews, and I really need to practice," she laughed and patted her belly instinctively.

Amir passed the baby carefully into Inbal's gentle embrace. Inbal looked lovingly at the baby. "Man, she's so cute!" she gushed. "You know what you're going to call her?"

"We have some ideas," Daria said.

"Can I see too?" I said and bent toward Inbal.

"Sure." Inbal smiled and slightly loosened her cradling embrace.

I stared at the baby, and I knew immediately that my suspicions were correct.

Inbal was holding Nofar.

My Nofar.

Who was now Daria's.

She was always Amir's, and now she had another mother. During my new life, I'd had quite a few moments of déjà vu. I didn't always know if they were real memories of my past or a normal feeling of déjà vu that every person experiences from time to time. Now, I was confused. The original Nofar, my daughter in my former life, was a genetic combination of Amir and me. How could Amir and Daria have the exact same child? I once read that children are often more like their father. When Nofar was my daughter, opinion was divided: Some people had argued that she looked like me, and some had said she looked like Amir. I thought she didn't look like either of us.

I looked at her in horror. For the first time, I saw the similarities between her and Amir. Were his genes so strong that they overwhelmed both my genes and Daria's genes? My Nofar was created despite the birth control measures I took. Was Amir's sperm so dominant that he beat the contraception and definitively established the identity of the baby?

"Is something wrong?" Daria asked, noticing my stunned look.

"Nope," I lied. "I'm just stunned that you're a mother, that you have a baby girl," I said after a long and heavy silence. I found it difficult to find an excuse for my stunned look.

"Yes," she said. "It's hard to believe."

"She's so tiny," Inbal continued to coo. I wanted to be sure. After all, all babies look alike... maybe it was all in my head. I went to Inbal and the little baby and pulled at her clothes gently. My Nofar had a birthmark between her right shoulder and her neck.

"What are you doing?" Inbal protected the baby.

"Nothing," I apologized. "I thought there was something there."

"Where?" Inbal asked and pulled her one-piece aside, which allowed me to see Nofar's birthmark in all its glory.

"Nofar," I whispered.

"What did you say?" Daria asked.

"Nothing," I apologized. "I was just confused."

"I thought you said Nofar," Daria said in shock. "That's weird, because Amir really likes that name and that's what we think we'll call her."

"It really is a nice name," Inbal said and passed little Nofar to her current mother.

"What do you think, Amiri?" Daria turned to my former husband.

"You know I love that name," he smiled.

"So, there you are, then - you guys are first to know," Daria declared. "Our baby is called Nofar."

"Congratulations," Inbal said.

"Yes, congrats," I said almost in a whisper.

"Well," Daria said to Nofar in a babyish voice, "Let's see if you'll finally agree to nurse from your mother."

I couldn't tell her now she wouldn't. Nofar wouldn't nurse. It was just not worth the effort and guilt. Now I understood that Nofar simply didn't want to breastfeed. She had no problem with my milk, specifically.

On the way home, I asked Inbal. "When did you say your due date is?"

"Mid-February," she said in surprise. "Why do you ask?"

"No reason..." I pondered for a minute. "Do you know what you're having?"

"Probably a boy." She smiled and stroked her stomach with excitement.

Roy, Asi and Daria's son in my previous life, was born on 18th February 2008. I remembered the date because it was also my mother's birthday.

I waited impatiently for February. I was anxious to find out if the 'new' Roy, in my current life, would be completely identical to the Roy in my previous life. The thought filled me with horror. Biologically, there may be some similarity, but the genes of a different spouse would surely result in a different baby, at least in some respect. I spent my time until the birth watching Nofar. Unlike in her previous life with me, her picture was constantly taken, and I got a photographic update almost daily. With every day that passed, my hope that I was wrong and that this was a new Nofar faded away. She was exactly the same Nofar. Once again, just like last time, despite Daria's efforts to hide it, Nofar wasn't an easy child, and, once again, she preferred her father over anyone else.

It was over eleven years since I'd woken up in the hospital – again - into a new life. I was used to the strange reality of my life, but Nofar's birth was a far cry from what I'd known so far. Because I had made different choices in my new life, my life wasn't an exact repeat of the previous one. I'd married another man, and I'd chosen a different career and therefore the sequence of events and experiences in my new life were not identical to those of my previous life. My sisters and other relatives made similar choices to those I remembered from my former life, and, therefore, they had the same children and grandchildren I had known in my former life. But Daria, Inbal and I had switched partners, so a 'replay' of offspring seemed like science fiction to me.

On February 18th 2008, Asi and Inbal had a baby boy. Everyone except me was impressed by the fact that the child was born weighing over 9 pounds. Roy weighed exactly the same. The circumcision was held, like last time, a week late, because the baby suffered from neonatal jaundice. Inbal and Asi named the child Roy. I was as surprised by the choice of name as I was that he was the exact same child. I remembered that in my previous life, Daria chose the name, but now she wasn't the child's mother. I guessed a person's name was given to him in a more mystical way than I'd thought.

Unlike Nofar, who was my daughter in my previous life, I didn't really remember Roy. I certainly couldn't say that they were definitely identical. The realization that this was the exact same Roy came to me over time. In my previous life, I saw Roy mainly in pictures Daria constantly sent out. Most of the time, I simply deleted the pictures before even looking at them, but I remembered that Roy had a funny shock of black hair, even as a newborn. I recognized him from miles away. Among the many bald babies, he stood out like a lump of coal on a bed of white ice. As time passed, the little doubt I had disappeared; he was exactly the same child.

After Roy's birth, I realized in the coming months that I was supposed to get pregnant. If, in my new life, the fathers got exactly the same offspring they'd had in their previous lives, then Coral, David and Inbal's eldest daughter, was to be born to David and me at the end of 2008. I didn't know if I even wanted to have children in the current round of my life and now faced a dilemma. I could avoid a pregnancy by using the safest contraceptive around: abstinence. Although David's sex drive was much higher than Amir's, I could come up with various excuses for two to three months. Since Nofar was conceived while I was on the pill, I knew that only avoiding sex would prevent me becoming pregnant with Coral. Was prevention of certain pregnancy the same as having an abortion? I'd considered aborting Nofar when I was first pregnant with her. Now, I knew in advance that I might be pregnant... I knew the daughter I thought I'd have. The thought that I was standing in the way of Coral's right to come into the world troubled me, and I decided I wouldn't stop her from being born, not actively, anyway. I didn't stop taking the pills, but nor did I abstain from sex with David.

A few weeks later, on Independence Day of that year, Daria, Inbal, Amir, Asi, David and I got together again to watch the fireworks show. Like last time, we were hosted by Asi, but this time his co-host was

Inbal. Contrary to our previous life, in which Asi and Daria had lived in a luxury apartment in north Tel Aviv, in our current lives Inbal chose to invest the fortune Asi made in his father's import business in a house in a small suburb near Kfar Saba. Asi and Inbal's new home did not in any way resemble the designer space that Asi and Daria had made together. The house itself was, indeed, a great piece of real estate that I knew I couldn't afford in the coming years, but it was much warmer and cozier than the stylish apartment I remembered. The innovative, designer furniture was gone, to make way for simple styles; drapes in bright colors graced the windows, and souvenirs that Asi and Inbal had collected during their many visits to the Far East were scattered throughout the house. In contrast to the immaculate cleanliness of Daria and Asi's apartment, Asi and Inbal's home was a mess, as befits a house where a baby was growing up. Inbal didn't bother to hide the mounds of laundry piled up in the living room. The kitchen was a mess and a variety of toys were scattered around the house. I remembered that last time, with Roy sitting on the bouncer. This time, he was cradled against Inbal's body in a carrier made of fabric. I approached her and looked at little Roy. I had no doubt. This was the same Roy I remembered. Daria and Amir were sitting on the couch watching Nofar, who, once again, was eyeing Roy's toys scattered on the floor.

"Sorry about the mess," Inbal apologized with a smile.

"I didn't expect anything else," I laughed.

Nofar picked up a sponge ball and put it in her mouth. Daria snatched the ball from her. "She's putting everything in her mouth at the moment," she apologized. Again, Nofar burst into tears and stopped only after Amir picked her up in his arms.

"It's okay," Inbal said apologetically, not wanting Nofar to cry over her son's toy. "She can chew it if she wants.We don't live in a pharmacy."

"Roy's still very small," Daria said. "I don't know if it's okay for him to come into contact with other children's saliva."

"He'll have to get used to it at some point," I smiled. "He'll be going to kindergarten before long," I repeated the sentence I'd said last time.

"That's right," Inbal laughed. Although she could afford to stay home with Roy until he finished high school, she believed that children should spend at least part of the day with their peers.

The fireworks began, and we looked up at the colorful sky. Amir was holding Nofar, who pointed in amazement at the bright flashes of light. Roy began to cry hysterically, and Inbal took him inside. David stood beside me and looked at the sky with curiosity. I clung to him. I wanted him to lay his hand on my shoulder. My memory of him embracing Inbal and looking at fireworks was engraved in my mind, and I wanted to recreate it.

"Is something wrong?" he asked as I rubbed my shoulder against his.

"No..." I said sadly. "I just thought it would be nice if you hugged me."

"Of course," he smiled, kissed me on the cheek and took me into his arms.

Now we were as I remembered, but the insult was already there. Why didn't he hug me as he'd hugged Inbal? Why did I have to ask him?

I squinted at Amir. In my previous life, the comparison between him and David wasn't fair. David was, and is, an amazing man, muscular and sexy. Amir had let himself go when we were married, and I was surprised that, with Daria, he looked much better, though still not as good as David, but it wasn't a fair competition. David had to stay in shape because of his work. The beer belly Amir had in our previous lives hadn't recreated itself; his hair was thinning, but much less than I remembered. I remembered my mother pestering me often, saying I should take better care of Amir, and I always got angry at her for giving me medieval advice. I wished I'd listened to her more. I figured Daria, who always liked people to look their best, made sure Amir watched his weight better than I did, and the results definitely showed. A few minutes later, the fireworks ended and we sat around the dinner table on the porch to eat the steaks Asi had cooked.

"Excellent," Inbal said with pleasure.

"Thank you," Asi flashed a loving smile at his wife. I watched him. He, too, was not the person he had been in his previous life. In his former life, he was thinner, but always looked worried and angry. Daria had encouraged him to wear tight tops, designer jeans, luxury shoes and hair gel. With Inbal, he was dressed in a simpler, more relaxed manner. I was amazed to see him wearing sandals. I'd never seen his feet before. I was happy Daria had failed to force Amir to wear metrosexual style clothes.

"Enjoy." Daria smiled at Inbal with a starving look. She hadn't touched the steak Asi had served her. Since she'd finally lost all the baby weight, she wasn't going to gain another ounce.

"You're looking good," Daria told me.

"Thank you," I smiled.

"Did you do something to your hair?" Daria frowned.

"Are you wearing makeup? There's something different about you."

"Nope," I shrugged.

Asi returned from the kitchen with a bottle of wine and started to pour everyone a glass. When he reached mine, I didn't stop him, but David quickly said, "Maybe you shouldn't."

"You're pregnant?" Daria blurted out in a demonstration of tactlessness.

I took a deep breath and said, "Yes!"

"Wow! Rose!" Daria jumped up and hugged me. "That's great. Stand up so we can get a better look at you."

I stood up and rubbed my stomach. "I'm not showing yet," I apologized. "Early days..."

"What week?" Inbal inquired.

"Tenth," I smiled at her. She came to me, and we hugged a long and loving embrace, just like we did when she announced she was pregnant with Coral.

"So you don't know what you're having yet," she said.

"No," I lied. I already knew what I'd name my daughter, who was her daughter in my other life.

.

CHAPTER 16

It was totally different expecting Coral than it had been with Nofar. The pregnancy symptoms didn't knock me sideways this time as they had with Nofar. I had less nausea, less indigestion, less bloating. I felt much better. I was glowing, as many told me. But beyond the physical symptoms that were different, there was one fundamental difference: This time, I was prepared for the pregnancy. While David was surprised that I got pregnant whilst still on the pill, I was far less surprised. It happened to me in my previous life, and I was expecting Coral anyway. David was hoping for a boy, but I knew that I wouldn't fulfill his wish. In the first ultrasound, the doctor thought he saw a penis. David was thrilled, but I knew the doctor was wrong. At the next test, the doctor told us what I'd already known before I even got pregnant.

During my first pregnancy, with Nofar, I was immersed in grief, crying for my career, which I felt I'd destroyed with my own hands. This time, I had the job I aspired to and had already managed to gain some years of experience. I had no doubt that pregnancy would hold up my career, but I knew this time it would be just a small bump on the way and not a dead end. Eagerly, I awaited Coral's arrival. I remembered her as a sweet and incredibly easy baby. I decided that, this time, everything was going to be different. This time, I was going to accept motherhood and treat my daughter with patience and love.

Coral's birth was quick and easy, a totally different experience from Nofar's birth. When the nurse put little Coral on my stomach, I hugged her and kissed her warmly. I was 'normal' this time around. No nurse looked at me accusingly. David was happy despite his hope for a boy and never stopped hugging our little girl and showing her off to everyone he knew and even to those he didn't. He claimed that she looked exactly like me, and I chuckled to myself. In a different life, she was Inbal's daughter. David wanted to call her Ruth and didn't understand my fixation with the name Coral. Only when his older sister fawned over the name Coral did he give in, and the baby received the same name she'd had sixteen years earlier.

My first few days as a mother were incomparable with those in my previous life. It was so pleasant. This time, my little daughter nursed from me greedily, and I felt that, this time, she wanted me and I wanted her. This time, I wasn't surprised by the pregnancy, the birth or the demands of parenting. I knew exactly what it meant to be a mother to a baby. David was amazed by all the knowledge I had and the professionalism I demonstrated while taking care of our daughter. He never stopped praising me. From the first moment, I knew how to hold the child correctly, feed her, clothe her, and bathe her, like I did in the past. "You're amazing," he whispered to me over and over again. He was afraid it would be difficult for me because he wasn't at all sure I'd wanted to be a mother.

The problem was that, while I remembered just how to manage infant care, I still didn't have a way with children. In the first months, the baby only needed me like she'd need a nurse. I only had to feed her, wash her and change her diapers. Once I had to communicate with her, I found the same difficulties occurring. I didn't talk in a babyish voice, I couldn't understand Coral's various different stares, and I was terribly bored from sitting with her for days and playing baby games.

I went back to work at the end of the three-month maternity leave approved by law. Around me, a lot of eyebrows were raised over the speed with which I returned to work, but I knew from past experience that two more months with my daughter wouldn't change the fact that I hated sitting at home with a baby. I really loved Coral and realized now that I'd really loved Nofar, too, and that I'd blamed something on her that was really just ingrained in me. I thought I didn't love her enough, but I just didn't like being a mother. Beyond the fact that I didn't enjoy sitting at home, the main reason I returned to work so quickly was because I knew I'd be pregnant again in no time. Adi was born just over a year after Coral.

David's sex drive was quite different from Amir's. I remembered Amir claiming "all guys are the same." While in some respects he was right. I had various disputes with David that sounded remarkably similar to those I had with Amir, but when it came to the bedroom, there was nothing in common between the two men in my past and present life. With both, I enjoyed myself, but with Amir I felt I had too little sex, while with David I had too much. I assumed it was related to both their natural sex drive and the fact that David was more physically active. Amir could go weeks without having sex, and David was frustrated if a week went by without us having sex at least twice. Once Coral was born, I told him he'd have to settle for once a week because I was just exhausted. David was constantly bringing up the subject, and when I became pregnant again, when Coral was less than five months old, I wasn't at all surprised. In my previous life, I was jealous of Inbal because her husband wanted her so much, and in my present life, I envied Daria because she could have some peace and quiet. I realized that sex drive has nothing to do with love, because I was sure that David loved me very much, but his need for sex wasn't related to me. It was just his physiological structure.

In July of that year, we met with Daria, Inbal, Amir and Asi for Amir's birthday. As a present, I bought him a book I remembered that he enjoyed very much in my previous life.

"Have you read this book already?" I asked as he unwrapped it.

"Not yet... I've heard about this book. I read another one by this author, which I didn't really like," he said and began to read the exchange note that came with the book.

"Read it!" I ordered him. "I'm sure you'll love it."

"If you say so," he smiled, and Daria watched the little intimate conversation that developed between us with a menacing look.

The waiter came over and took the orders. "Would you like to order wine?" he asked.

"Sure," Amir said. He was an avid wine lover and

ordered us a quality bottle of wine.

When the waiter moved around us to pour the wine, I signaled to him that I wasn't interested. Daria looked at me, stunned, and when the waiter disappeared, she said, "Don't tell me you're pregnant again!"

"I am," I smiled sheepishly.

"How old is Coral? Six months?" She tried to calculate in her mind.

"Seven."

"You're not normal!"

"Why isn't she normal?" Inbal chimed in. I knew she was jealous, not because I had more sex than her, but because she desperately wanted a second child. "The best thing is to have children with a small age gap between them. That way, they grow up together," she said. I wanted to comfort her and tell her that she'd soon be pregnant for the second time. In fact, she might have already been expecting Shira, Daria and Asi's second child in their previous life. I could even encourage her and tell her she'd be the only one of us to embrace a third child.

"It wasn't planned," I lied. Not only was it planned, I actually knew about it in advance. "But I'm happy it happened. I want to complete our family as soon as possible." I smiled, and now it was Inbal's turn to look at me with a stunned stare. I wasn't sure if she was shocked by the fact that I didn't want more than two children, or the fact that I saw having children as a task I wanted to be finished with, and as not the essence of life.

"It's lucky you went back to work so fast," Daria added. "At first, I thought you were pushing it, but now I've no doubt it was one very lucky choice! If you'd extended your maternity leave, I don't know if there would have been any point in you going back to work." Daria noted a fact that I'd been aware of since the day Coral was born.

"That's true," Inbal said. I knew she was the most shocked at the speed with which I went back to work.

At the office, the fact that I'd returned to work after only three months wasn't so extraordinary. Plenty of lawyers didn't use the opportunity to extend their minimum maternity leave, and those who did so were not as career-driven as I was. Knowing that I'd be pregnant within a short time, I hadn't felt pressured to take on large cases. I saw the months that separated both of my maternity leaves as a time in which I worked to keep my job, nothing more. I planned to move my career forward after Adi's birth.

In the same period in my previous life, I'd just started work at Smart Green as chief bookkeeper. This time, my life was completely different: Then, I'd worked hard, trying to prove myself at all costs; now, I enjoyed the benefits that came with the flexibility associated with a mother's job. I had been so envious of David and Inbal's loving relationship, but now I was David's wife and I had nothing to be jealous of. The fact that I knew in advance about my second pregnancy really made my life easier. John Lennon was right when he said that life is what happens to you when you're busy making other plans. In my previous life I was busy planning, being disappointed and feeling jealous. Now I knew in advance what was going to happen, and I learned to live my life instead of thinking about what could have been.

I watched Daria and Amir, and Inbal and Asi, and saw surprising similarities between the relationships that Daria had with Asi and Inbal had with David. Just as Daria had controlled Asi, she now controlled Amir, the difference being that Amir knew better how stand up for himself. In addition, Inbal's relationship with Asi looked as warm and loving from the outside as her relationship with David. I realized that a spousal relationship doesn't depend solely on the connection between the two people, but also depends on each of them individually. Daria was an impatient control freak, and that was reflected in her relationships with both Asi and Amir. Inbal, however, was a loving and dedicated person who radiated warmth and love and each man who lived with her simply blossomed. David didn't wither with me, but in my memory, he was a happy and cheerful man when he lived with Inbal.

This comparison that my new life allowed offered me relief. Amir was wrong when he said, "Everyone's the same." Absolutely not! But there was no point in being jealous of others about things I couldn't control. I couldn't be Inbal. We didn't have the same personality - so there was no point in being jealous of her life with Asi, just as there was no point in being jealous of her life with David at the time. Now, I still couldn't help but be jealous of her ability to love, but I knew that I had traits that she lacked and the jealousy that drove me crazy in my previous life didn't return with such ferocity in my new life.

CHAPTER 17

Adi was born in January of 2010. I didn't remember the exact date of Adi's previous birth, but I assumed it was the same date exactly. David was disappointed that, once again, he didn't get a son, but he hoped for one "next time." I knew for certain that I wouldn't conceive again before September of 2012, and, to be honest, I had no intention of having another child. I was glad I was done with the baby making period of my life. I realized that I didn't enjoy parenting, no matter who the baby was. I just wasn't born to be a mother. If I hadn't known I was scheduled to give birth to Coral and Adi, I might not have had any children at all. I just didn't want to prevent them from entering this world. I had an advantage that no parent ever experienced in their life: I knew what it meant to be a parent before my daughters were even born. I had no doubt that many parents would give up parenting if they knew beforehand what the experience entails. Despite these feelings and although I felt that Coral and Adi were imposed on me in some mystical way, I didn't regret parenthood as much as I had in my previous life. Even though I knew I would never be Mother of the Year, I loved my kids and was glad I had a family. For David, anyway, there was no other option. It was obvious to him that we'd start a family, so, in that respect, I really had no other option.

We decided to mark Adi's birth with a small event. Little Coral turned one a few weeks before Adi's birth, so we combined two events into one little party at a restaurant we liked. Lior and Aya arrived late, so they had to sit with Inbal and Daria, instead of with the people from the office who were seated at a nearby table. In my present life, I had no social ties with Aya. The circumstances were not as they were in my previous life, and past experience had taught me that our friendship was destructive for me.

"Wow, what a snob!" Daria declared to me the next day.

"Who?" I asked.

"Come on..." she said with an impatient tone, "the two pompous people you sat us with."

"Lior and Aya?"

"Yes, Lior and Aya..." She pronounced Aya's name like she was going to vomit.

"They're actually a very nice couple." I defended them. They really were very positive people.

"I don't know..." She began to reconsider a little when she realized I didn't share her feelings. "She seemed cocky to me, and he was kind of a putz."

I agreed about Lior being a putz, but I didn't want to share my opinions with Daria. I didn't know when and where Daria might blurt out what I'd said about one of the partners of my firm. "I don't really know her," I lied.

I knew her very well, only not in my current life. "He's a partner at my firm."

"He's a partner?" she asked in amazement. "He looks very young."

"He's really young… he's simply a genius."

"Wow," she said. "I wouldn't have guessed. He looks like such a nerd… I was sure he's a bank clerk or something."

"He's not," I explained. "He's one of the best attorneys in his field."

"Okay…" she said humbly. Her theory proved to be false.

"Why do you think his wife's cocky?" I was curious. I remembered Aya well and arrogance wasn't one of her most prominent traits. If anything, she was generally modest about her successes.

"No reason," she replied, considering her thoughts again. "Amir mentioned a law that was being discussed in the Knesset about sanctioning employers of contract workers and she said it was discussed in the Finance Committee meeting this week and she was on the committee."

"Because she probably was."

"Really?"

"Yes, she's a lawyer who works in an office with a lot of lobbyists."

"Wow!" Daria realized she was way off track. "Then they really are a successful pair!"

"Absolutely."

In my previous life, I busied myself constantly with Aya and Lior's success and choosing to study law in my present life was rooted primarily in the fact that I wanted to be like Aya. Now I was a lawyer in a job just as respectable as Aya's, but I was still careful not to make personal contact with her. I didn't want my negative feelings to come back again. Now, I actually knew Lior better and already had enough negative feelings toward him: I felt he had been promoted because of me, and I didn't want to develop feelings of envy again regarding his wife. I had to admit to myself that I took evil pleasure in inviting Aya to our event in honor of Adi's birth. I knew Aya was struggling to conceive at that time, but I knew the advantage I had over her in the fertility department was temporary, and she was going to be pregnant soon, within a few months.

Daria's interest in Aya and Lior told me that it wasn't just me who found Lior and Aya a source of interest and jealousy. Daria, in her current life, could only boast her external appearance. This time, she didn't enjoy living in the top hundredth percentile, and envy was burning her inside. I was glad I wasn't there this time. I felt that my present life was in my hands, under control.

Again, after Adi's birth, I returned to work immediately after my maternity entitlement. As long as Adi was nursing, I had to work limited hours, but when she was six months old I stopped breastfeeding her and went back to work full time - and then some. I remembered Inbal still nursing Coral well after her first birthday, and I knew that, this time, Coral's and Adi's diets wouldn't include my milk. I knew now that pregnancies and births were behind me, and I gave my all to work. To my great joy, I was surrounded by women who were as devoted to their careers as I was. None were concerned about the quantity and quality of family pictures in their offices. I didn't feel abnormal as I once had. To be honest, I didn't understand why most of them bothered to have children. The hours we spent with our families dwindled to weekends only. I often stayed at the office until late at night, and almost every day I came home when Coral and Adi were already asleep. My salary allowed me to hire a part-time nanny who watched over the girls when David worked his shifts at the fire station. Since I spent most of the day at the office with people whose priorities in life were similar to mine, I didn't often hear the criticism about my life that my family and friends might have. My lifestyle drove my mother crazy. She didn't go to work until my youngest sister was seven, so a woman who worked for days without even seeing her little girls - sometimes even on weekends - was abnormal in her eyes. Tamar, my older sister, was married and was a mother of three herself, and she couldn't understand me. From Nurit, my little sister, I got a little more encouragement, but probably only because she was still single, which helped me a lot because she babysat for my daughters sometimes.

Daria didn't bring the issue up often. I assumed she was uncomfortable criticizing me about a field she'd failed in. She wasn't a devoted mother to Nofar, just as I wasn't in my previous life. Because I remembered that she wasn't particularly maternal in her previous life either, I realized that it had nothing to do with Nofar herself. In her previous life, Daria had a whole fleet of nannies and maids who'd raised her children. Now that she had to take care of her child herself, she did so grudgingly. She had no patience like Inbal had, for example. Inbal, who was now married to the richest person in our group, hadn't hired a nanny to raise Roy and Shira for her. I was happy for her because I knew that in two years' time, she was going to become the mother of Galia, the sweet little baby I met on the day I had my second accident. Inbal never talked about my poor parenting and my non-presence at home, but I knew that she didn't approve of it. Whenever she took an interest in me and my daughters and saw how little I was involved in their lives, I saw her eyes sadden. She felt pain for my daughters. I also hurt, but I knew that I couldn't give them more. I felt that by bringing them into the world, I'd already done my part.

The criticism that hurt me most was David's. He was deeply disappointed with the way I raised my daughters. Before I became pregnant with Coral, I'd told him I wasn't sure if I wanted to be a mother. He pleaded with me to allow him to become a father. I explained to him that I wanted a career that wouldn't leave much room for children, but he insisted and promised that he would agree to raise our children, just as long as we had some to raise. I guess the fact that I brought two girls into the world with such a short gap in between, and that I'd agreed to freeze my career for a year and a half confused him a little. He thought I'd change my mind and fall in love with motherhood. Soon, he was disappointed to discover that I felt I'd kept my part of the deal. I'd brought two daughters into the world and started our family, but once I stopped breastfeeding my younger daughter, I went straight back to where I'd left off before the birth. David knew how to live modestly. In their previous lives, Inbal and David lived off his modest salary as a firefighter, so I knew that his pleas to cut my working hours down, even at the expense of our financial quality of life, weren't just true in theory. In my previous incarnation, I lived frugally, and I knew I could get along with less, but I didn't want to compromise as I'd had to in my previous life. Now, my salary at Lifschitz, Cohen & Co. was more than double what I'd earned with Smart Green. I enjoyed my professional success and enjoyed our financial security. After all, I already knew from my former life that, even if I came home early every day, I wasn't going to be a very good mother. I preferred to focus on what I was good at.

I was a good lawyer. That, nobody doubted. Not my family, not my friends nor my colleagues. The senior partners valued me and told me more than once that they saw me as a future partner.

I was good.

But not great.

They appreciated my work, but I never got admiring looks like those Lior received. Lior wasn't alone. There were several lawyers like him, most of them older than me, but some new young lawyers began to appear and managed to grab the limelight while I remained in the shadows. In most cases, my knowledge and diligence exceeded theirs. I'd been a lawyer for nearly five years, most of them in the Cohen, Lifshitz & Co. tax department. I worked full time plus extra hours, and most of my hours I spent reading and studying verdicts and memorizing sections of the law. I had an enormous knowledge that very few people in my field had and therefore I made a good salary. However, I didn't belong to the elite group, a small number of lawyers who received superstar treatment. Most of them couldn't compete with my knowledge, but every one of them had an ability that I found hard to develop - they knew how to bend the law, speak convincingly to clients and judges and compete with other lawyers. They knew how to lie and manipulate. I didn't do it well enough. I felt I was already kind of living one big lie because of my previous life, which occasionally forced me to pretend. I had no more room for lies in my life.

Before I started studying law, my mother tried to discourage me from that profession. She claimed that I didn't know to lie well enough and that, in order to be a good lawyer, you must know to lie. "You need to constantly be an actor appearing before a changing audience," she'd said. "And you don't know how to act at all," she'd added. I thought she was wrong. I was, indeed, a poor actress, but I didn't believe you had to be a liar and a manipulator to succeed in court. I found out that I was wrong; to reach the summit, you must know to lie. This reality hurt me, because, again, I felt that there was no reward given to me for the time and effort I invested, that slackers' voices were better heard because they knew how to speak convincingly. I wanted them to have more appreciation for knowledge and professionalism. I came across more and more cases in which solutions that were too creative caused more problems than if the client had simply followed the law. Various tax planning created in the minds of the firm's superstars, even some designed by Lior, failed to withstand the test of time. The Israeli Tax Authorities didn't always accept the plans, and the cases returned to us for a second round of discussions in the courts with the tax authorities, so that their work was in vain. In some cases, I calculated that if they weren't trying to be so clever and bend the rules, then the client would have been better off by simply not paying the firm to reduce his tax bill. I once dared to present the data I'd found to one of the partners. The result was that I picked up cases in which the communication with the customers was limited. I was an amazing source of knowledge, but they didn't want me to talk with customers.

I felt that, even though I'd chosen a new path in my life, the sense of déjà vu was strong. Just like in my previous life, the field of law didn't put enough emphasis on professionalism, knowledge and efficiency, just like the field of finance. Senior jobs were filled by smooth-tongued people regardless of their professional skills, which were often insufficient in my opinion. The difference was that, as a lawyer, they gave me a little more respect for my knowledge and my salary was much higher, which somewhat quieted my feelings of bitterness and jealousy. I knew it could be worse.

When Saul asked me to join him for a meeting with a new client, I was surprised. I wasn't used to being invited to meetings, certainly not first meetings with clients. It soon became clear that the customer had been referred by the department that dealt with white-collar crimes, so they needed a lawyer with a background in accounting. On the way to the boardroom, Saul briefed me and informed me that this was a relatively small company as opposed to the many large companies we worked with, but it was a subsidiary of a giant American corporation, which had asked us to handle a scandal discovered in the company. Embezzlement of over a million dollars was at the root of it. The full circumstances were not yet clear, but the story was discovered by chance as the result of an unexpected income tax audit.

I went into the conference room full of expectations. The case sounded intriguing, and I was happy to lead a case in front of a client and not stay behind the scenes with the other lawyers. When I walked into the conference room, my new client was sitting with his back to me, and the lawyer from the other department said, "Oh, here's the lawyer I told you about." The client turned around expectantly, and I was amazed to discover that my new client was none other than Gideon Zohar, my former boss at Smart Green.

He extended his hand to me, but I was too stunned to react. His hand was almost back at his side when I finally pulled myself together and extended my hand. "Very nice to meet you," I said confidently. "Rose Lerner-Evrony."

"It's very nice to meet you too," he said. "Gideon Zohar."

We sat down and exchanged business cards. I glanced at the business card he handed me, and I was amazed to find that I still remembered Smart Green's phone number by heart.

The lawyer asked Gideon to describe the company to me. It was, of course, completely unnecessary, but I pretended, as I was now used to doing in my present life. When Gideon finished, the lawyer described the sequence of events that led Gideon and Smart Green to our office. I knew with complete certainty that the incident occurred due to whoever filled the role I had left in my previous life. In my time, the company's books were in perfect order and we had no unexpected audits from the Israeli Tax Authorities.

"In March of this year, Smart Green filed its tax return for the previous tax year, as they do every year," my colleague explained. "The company's taxable income is relatively small and therefore the company demanded a refund of their advance tax payments paid during this year."

"And that's why the tax authorities were knocking at their door asking for an audit." I smiled knowingly.

"Yes."

I glanced in Gideon's direction. I saw he was impressed.

"At first, the management, led by Gideon here, wasn't

afraid of the audit, but soon they discovered irregularities in various accounts and the suspicion is that the chief bookkeeper embezzled the company's money."

"The accounts auditor didn't notice the embezzlement during the audit?"

"No, the subject was reviewed. It's possible the auditors had something to do with the embezzlement too."

I knew that wasn't possible.

"I don't think so," Gideon said. "I trust them. They may not have completed a sufficiently good audit, but they're not thieves."

His words warmed my heart. I had no doubt that the office where I spent most of my previous working life was staffed by honest people.

"Anyway, since the auditors missed the fraud, they're not sitting with us today, so our examination will be impartial."

"I understand," I said, and immediately added, "What about the company accountant? Did he not notice the illegal actions of the chief bookkeeper?"

"We don't have an accountant," Gideon said.

"Why is that?" I asked innocently.

"I saw no need to employ an accountant. For years, I had an excellent chief bookkeeper." I thought of the amazing Shoshana. "She did a great job. She retired two years ago and we hired Tomer for the job in her place. At first I thought he was an excellent solution for the company. He'd just finished his internship in accounting."

"So he's a CPA?" I interrupted.

"Yes."

"I don't understand," I lied. "So he's the accountant then, is he not?"

"No," Gideon said with an embarrassment that I savored. He was – finally - embarrassed by his own definition of the role he forced on me in my previous life. "I didn't think there was any need to apply that job title, which costs more money, when for years the job description was chief bookkeeper." Now, the cat was out of the bag. What I had suspected for years was now a fact.

The other attorney didn't understand why I was taking so much interest in the job descriptions and asked Gideon to continue the story about the embezzlement. It turned out that Tomer, who came from an accounting firm I didn't know, approached work with a lot of motivation. He was trying to prove himself by initiating business processes in the company. Gideon was initially very impressed by Tomer's initiatives, but in time he realized that Tomer was neglecting the ongoing work in favor of long meetings with customers and suppliers. "He was supposed to make sure the company's books were balanced, that adjustments were made to various accounts, and not to do business," Gideon said. After some suppliers complained that their payments didn't arrive on time, Gideon had to put Tomer in his place and, according to Gideon's assessment, that's when the embezzlement started, more or less.

I dove into the case with astonishing speed, due in large to the fact that I knew the company and its financial report well from my past. I was able to disclose how Tomer embezzled money and significantly reduce the scope of the embezzlement and the damage done with the tax authorities. Gideon was deeply impressed by my abilities and professionalism. He even invited me to come and work in his company as the CFO. The offer was very flattering, but I didn't consider it,not for a moment. Gideon's management style, which was familiar to me from many other places, disgusted me. Again and again I saw dedicated employees sidelined in favor of new stars who were put at the top, often lacking the training and relevant experience.

CHAPTER 18

In August 2011, I knew that Daria would give birth to my beloved second son. I knew the exact birth date, which was almost a month before the expected delivery date. I wanted to be as far away as possible from Daria. I found it hard to see her with Amir and even with Nofar, so I knew that seeing her hugging my favorite little Tom would be impossible for me. David was surprised by the fact that, for the first time in our lives, I initiated a vacation. I booked us all a luxurious, two-week vacation in Holland and Belgium. We flew the day before Tom was born and returned after the circumcision ceremony. I was saved. Daria couldn't be angry with me, because I couldn't have known that she'd give birth at the beginning of the ninth month. I was happy. I was far away from my former son, even though I knew I'd have to see him with his new mother at some point.

David mistook the long vacation as an omen. He hoped that the wonderful family time we spent together would make me reduce my time at work, so I'd be present more at home. It didn't happen. In the past years, my marriage to David had begun to crack. This was due to all the regular reasons that arise from a routine life, but, in our case, we each had a different approach to life, which caused the cracks to expand into deep grooves. David was a devoted family man who jealously guarded the sanctity of private time, while I was a devoted career woman who spent every free moment developing professionally. The reality of my life forced me to be a private person. I was afraid all the time that the secret of my former life would be exposed while David was a friendly and open person. I was very well-educated; I had a double degree in law and accounting and on top of that, an MBA in business management, and I kept up with my professional development. David, in contrast, barely completed his degree and had no need or desire to study for another. To be honest, it didn't bother me that I was more educated than he was. In my eyes, David was a very smart guy; he used his spare time to develop a variety of hobbies. He read dozens of books, and his general knowledge was greater than mine. Nonetheless, I had a feeling that the environment was telling David and me that there was something off in a relationship where the woman was better qualified than the man (at least on paper).

Our sex life also became worn out. In the past, we'd slept together at least twice a week, but now the average had dropped dramatically, not because of a lack of desire on David's part, or even on my part. I was just less present and a lot more tired. Over the years, David stopped begging. He felt he was forcing himself on me. More than once, I compared the relationship I had with Amir to my relationship with David. I had to admit to myself that Amir suited me better. I loved them both equally, and I was more attracted to David, but there were more connection points between Amir and me. That's why it was so hard to see Tom with Amir and his other mother. In my previous life, I was jealous of Daria because of her wealth. Now, I enjoyed greater prosperity, but still envied her. I missed Amir.

I temporarily escaped meeting Tom, but not for long. Inbal organized a family trip to the north for all three families during October. The trip was scheduled for the week of Sukkot, so I couldn't find refuge in work. David waited impatiently for the weekend while I didn't stop praying I'd get sick unexpectedly.

A week before the long-awaited trip, Yom Kippur came. David and I were not religious peopleand this holiday had never held special meaning for us in the past, but over the years, David started to find some comfort in religion and tradition. He didn't become religious and didn't believe he would, but I guess the different holidays celebrated at Coral's kindergarten lit his dormant Jewish spark. He asked me to light Shabbat candles every Friday, we made *kiddush* and began to add more fun traditions to our lives that we hadn't bothered to do in the past, when we were just a couple. I wasn't surprised when David decided to go to the *Kol Nidre* prayer on the eve of Yom Kippur and to *Neila* at the end. I went into the women's section at the end of the holiday, my head wrapped in a white scarf, listening to the sound of the *shofar*. Coral was next to David in the men's section, and I carried little Adi in my arms. I knew that, for many people, the *shofar* awakens the soul, but I didn't feel anything. I enjoyed the special atmosphere and tranquility that fell upon the whole congregation, but I didn't think that my soul was undergoing refinement.

When we left the synagogue, I noticed that something was wrong with David. He wasn't his usual self. He hugged our daughters and me with tears in his eyes. The prayers and the *shofar* touched his soul. He was preoccupied all evening, and I began to worry that this religious side of him was getting too serious.

When the girls were asleep, I sat down in the living room. He sat with a book. I watched him.He just stared at the book. His eyes didn't move and for long minutes he didn't even turn the page.

"Is something wrong?" I finally asked.

He put his book down, closed his eyes and said, almost like a breath, "Yes."

"What?" I asked anxiously. "Something happen at the synagogue?"

"No... I mean, yes... at the synagogue, I realized something."

"What?" I asked impatiently. I was afraid he was going to tell me he was becoming religious.

"I want you to know that I love you." He was starting to annoy me, but I let him continue his monologue. "I've loved you since I was sixteen years old, which means half of my life… you're my soul mate."

I smiled. It had been years since we'd exchanged such dramatic declarations of love, and it was nice to hear.

"You have to believe me," he continued, "you're the only one for me. There will be no other."

"And there never was," I said with a smile.

"Well, that's what I'm trying to say..." he said, wiping the grin off my face at once. "There was someone…"

I looked at him, stunned. I couldn't utter a word. Since I'd questioned him about our history before my birst accident, I knew that I was his first, as he was mine, and I assumed that this was also true in our present lives. I was wrong. Not everything was the same in my new life. He'd cheated on me.

I remained silent and he continued in a choked voice, "Today, in the synagogue, I realized I couldn't keep it inside anymore. You have to believe me that nothing's happening right now."

"But there was... " I said softly.

"Yes," he looked down, "there was."

"When?" I asked after a long pause.

"In reality, nothing really 'happened.'" David made imaginary quotation marks with his hands when he said the word happened.

"So did it or didn't it?" I said angrily. "You're starting to annoy me."

"Something began..." he began to ponder. He searched for the right words, but I had no patience to wait for the right words.

"Did you fuck her?" I asked angrily.

"No," he said in embarrassment.

"Make out with her?"

"What is 'making out 'really?" He pleaded ignorance.

"Jesus, David! Come on, who are you - Bill Clinton?" I asked and he laughed involuntarily. "It's not funny. Did you kiss? Hug?"

"Yes," he said, and I opened my eyes wide in surprise, "but only once."

"What do you mean 'only once'? You saw a sexy woman walking down the street, then hugged her and kissed her? That kind of 'once'?" I asked cynically. It was clear that this wasn't the case.

"No, it wasn't like that," he said with a pleading look. "Please... calm down."

"I'm finding that hard."

"So try to listen to me."

We were silent. He looked at me and waited for me to speak. "Come on... talk!" I ordered him.

"Rose, for years I've been telling you this life is difficult for me. I find it hard raising our little girls alone."

"You're not raising them alone," I interrupted. "I do my bit, and I also pay for Shula, who helps you a lot." Shula was the nanny.

"True, but it's always bothered me that we aren't together enough. We're not a family enough. We're not a couple enough. Even before Coral came along, I often felt like a bachelor... I'd come home to an empty house. Now I feel like a single parent, but I'm not. I have you, the woman of my life, who's constantly at work."

"David," I interrupted again, "we've had this conversation a dozen times in the past... You knew in advance what you were getting into. I'll also remind you that before Coral and Adi were born, you promised that my career wouldn't be compromised and that you'd be the parent who raised them and took care of them. You didn't get a pig in a poke."

"You're right, but life's dynamic. I couldn't predict how I'd feel... I didn't know in advance that I'd be so frustrated."

"So you were frustrated and looking for someone to comfort you?" I tried to get to the point.

"Absolutely not," he protested. "I really wasn't looking, and you know full well that when I'm not at work, I'm at home with the girls. It just happened, and the fact that I was frustrated by what happens between us didn't help. I know I was wrong, but if I was happy, I wouldn't even be in this situation... if you were here more, this wouldn't have happened."

"I'm glad you have someone to blame," I said

sarcastically. "I'm really very sorry that I made you cheat on me."

"I didn't cheat," he muttered.

"So what *did* you do?"

"A class of students came on a visit round the fire station. I was guiding the tour, and the teacher was very interested in the station." She was interested in other things, too, I noted to myself. "After the tour, she asked for my details so she could recommend me to her teacher friends at other schools."

"And you started talking..."

"Yes," he looked down. "We started talking. The conversation didn't have an intimate tone, at least, not at first. She also loves origami like I do, and we exchanged all kinds of special tricks for paper folding."

"But at some point, the conversation became intimate," I continued the story for him. It was corny and predictable.

"Yeah..."

"Is she married?"

"No, she's divorced with three children."

"How convenient. So when did your origami meetings become hot dates?"

"We barely met," David explained. "Mostly we talked on the phone and sent text messages."

"But you said you had physical contact," I reminded him, "although in my opinion, an emotional connection is also cheating."

"You're right..." he said painfully. "I'm so sorry."

"You said you had a physical encounter?"

"Once."

"What happened?"

"After weeks of non-stop conversations in which we poured our hearts out," (I figured he was whining about his witch of a wife who was never home, but I preferred not to ask), "she called me one night and asked to meet. She'd quarreled with her mother, the children were at their father's and she was lonely. I asked my mother to come and watch the girls, and I met her."

"At her house?"

"No way! I was afraid that something might happen -"

" But something did!"

"Right... we met at a small café, talked and talked and then walked around a bit. We sat in some dark garden, and before I knew it, I was hugging and kissing her."

I closed my eyes in pain. I knew where the story ended, but it was hard for me to imagine my spouse cheating on me with a desperate divorcée in a dark garden. I felt David near me. I recoiled, and he grabbed me by the shoulders. When I opened my eyes, he was really close to me.

"You have to believe me - within two minutes, I was out of there. I got up, I went and haven't had any contact with her since."

"How long ago was that?"

"Two months."

"Two months… and you haven't told me a thing."

"I didn't know what to say. I didn't do anything, really."

"You kissed her, embraced her, you had an emotional connection with her for weeks, maybe even months. To me, that's really not nothing."

"You're right," he said and looked down. "I've nothing more to say except to ask your forgiveness."

"I have to think about it," I said and left the house.

I had nowhere to go. There was no one I could pour my heart out to. I knew my mother would side with

David and claim that I had to sleep in the bed I'd made. My relationship with Daria and Inbal were long gone. We weren't at all close and, in any case, I wouldn't want to admit the failure of my marriage to anyone. I went to the beach. I sat down in a trendy bar and looked at the movement of the waves, mesmerized.

I thought.

I sat and thought for more than two hours until I got up and went home. I decided to forgive David, even though I didn't know if he'd told me the whole story and even though I knew I could never trust him again as I had in the past. He couldn't quite resist. He dragged himself voluntarily into a relationship that came to physical contact. This time, he'd stopped himself before having full sex, but what would happen next time?

On the other hand, even though I didn't like it one little bit, I couldn't ignore the fact that he had a point. I had to bear some responsibility, at least in part, for his loneliness and his need to find comfort.

David was waiting for me, wide awake, when I returned home. I explained to him that I was upset, but I was ready to move on, provided he would give me some breathing room until I could pull myself together.

He, of course, agreed to all the terms.

CHAPTER 19

A week after David's confession, we all went for the long weekend that Inbal had organized for us. We arrived at the kibbutz and Inbal was already waiting for us on the grass. She had surprises for the kids and was charged with positive energy like a scoutmaster. I, on the other hand, was very tired from a strenuous week at work and was still drained from David's confession a few days earlier. During the ride, David tried everything to entertain me and make me laugh, which only irritated me more. I wanted to save my 'everything's fine' face for the meeting with Daria and Inbal. I didn't have the energy or patience to pretend when it was just the two of us.

"You look completely exhausted," she said when she saw me approach her with Adi. "Perhaps you should give me this little munchkin!" She threw her hands forward, and Adi ran right into her inviting embrace "And go for a nap…"

"Are you crazy?" I said. "You have two small children

of your own - you want two more?" The question was rhetorical. I knew she'd like at least one more child, but I also knew she and Asi would soon be expecting again.

She smiled, defeated, and I sat next to her and hugged her. "I'm sure you'll have at least one more," I whispered. I wished I had a way to make her believe it.

David allowed me to go to rest and watched the children with Inbal. I watched them from a distance, when I was near our room. They were perfect together, just as they had been in my previous life. For one brief moment, I thought that maybe I shouldn't leave them alone... maybe the spark would return... but I knew David wouldn't dare do anything, especially after his confession and request for forgiveness, and Inbal was in love and happy with Asi.

When I woke up, Daria had arrived. We were excited to see each other - long time, no see.

"Where's Tom?" I asked nervously. My former son was already two months old, and I hadn't yet seen him yet.

"You haven't seen him yet!" Daria said reproachfully.

"True," I smiled a shy smile. Daria probably thought I was embarrassed by the fact that I hadn't made the effort to visit him yet, but really I was embarrassed that I had to lie again. I'd seen Tom before; his image was firmly etched in my memory.

"You'll have to wait. He and Amir were exhausted. They're sleeping now."

Half an hour later, Amir woke up and came out of their room with Tom cradled in his arms. I approached with tentative steps, my heart pounding fit to burst out of my chest.

I was going to see my beloved son again.

Tom was still sleepy. He opened and closed his eyes

and sweetly nestled into Amir. I looked at him with love. I had to hold myself back so I wouldn't cry. I wasn't an emotional woman, and I knew it would be hard for me to explain why I was so moved, meeting with Tom.

"Do you want to hold him?" Amir asked.

I shook my head. I couldn't speak. It was a perfect moment that seemed to be cut straight out of my previous life: just me, my husband and our son.

The moment ended when Daria approached us. "Why did you bring him out?" she scolded Amir. "He seems to be completely asleep."

"He started to cry," Amir apologized. "Anyway, wouldn't you rather he sleep later?"

"He's not at the stage where you limit his sleep, yet," she said, and grabbed my Tom from his hands in anger and went into their room.

I smiled sheepishly. He returned the sheepish smile.

"He really is a little sweetie," I finally said.

"Yes," he smiled with love. "He's such an easy baby," he told me what I already knew.

In the evening, after stuffing ourselves at the barbecue that Asi and David organized, we sat happily and laughed like we hadn't laughed in years. Inbal, Daria and I reminisced about our childhood. That is, Daria and Inbal brought back memories of our childhood, and I retold stories they had told me about our childhood, as if they were my memories. I couldn't remember anything of what had happened to me before I was sixteen years old. Daria, who was tired from breastfeeding, went to bed first, followed by Inbal and Asi.

Amir, David and I were left. David began to yawn and asked me if I was coming back to our room.

"I'm not really tired," I said. "I had a nap this afternoon," I reminded him.

"I'm not tired either," Amir joined me. He was also rested.

"Well, I'll leave you then." David said. "You have a key to the room? I like to lock up. Goodnight." He nodded to Amir.

"Yes," I said and let him go on his way.

I was alone with my ex-husband. I hadn't been alone with him even once in my new life.

I was thrilled.

"You want to take a stroll around the kibbutz?" Amir suggested, and I responded positively.

We set out. We left the kibbutz guest house complex. We passed the silent dining room and a deserted kindergarten. Some cats fled in panic as we passed by the slides. I jumped in terror and Amir hugged me briefly in a way that sent pleasant goosebumps down my back. We continued past the barn. The pungent smell made us walk faster, and we reached the edge of the kibbutz. A sign pointed the way to the viewing area for the lake, and Amir asked if I'd like to go there. "Why not?" I replied, and we set off in the direction of the arrow.

We got up there gasping. The road wasn't easy, and we hadn't taken any water with us.

We looked around the place with thirsty eyes until we found an old faucet. I bent down and drank eagerly. When I straightened up, I was soaked. Amir looked at me with amusement.

"I'm sure your prestigious clients would have a heart attack if they saw you like this," he said, grinning with his entire face.

"Why?"

"You look like a girl after a water fight, not a senior lawyer."

I laughed and went to sit on a bench facing the

stunning scenery of the lake. Amir joined me after satisfying his thirst, and we sat in silence. The moon was nearly full and there was a pleasant breeze. The viewing area was located in an abandoned garden and had an enchanting view of the lake, which hypnotized us for a long time.

"I want to thank you," Amir broke the silence and made my heart pound.

"What for?" I asked.

"The book you gave me for my birthday last year."

"Oh, God," I laughed. "You take your time with gratitude…"

"No…" he joined me laughing. "I just put it aside. I had no time and forgot about it… eventually, I read it only recently. Actually, I finished it a week ago, on Yom Kippur."

"Okay. Did you like it?"

"Very much."

"Yeah, I knew you'd love it," I said, careless of the words coming out of my mouth.

"How did you know?" he asked in amazement.

"I just guessed."

"Have you read it?"

"Yes." I'd read it more than sixteen years ago, in my previous life.

"And what did you think? Did you connect to it?"

The answer was not really. It was a good book, but I remembered that Amir was much more moved by it than I had been.

"The main character really moved me," I lied. I hadn't been able to understand the main character's dilemma, but Amir hadn't stopped talking about her for days. "Her dilemma, choosing between the two options available to her, moved me very much."

"Yeah, me too," Amir said with shining eyes.

"Did Daria read it? What did she say about it?"

"Daria barely reads," Amir said in a disappointed voice.

"You sound disappointed."

"A little," he said and made a face.

"Why?"

"As the years pass by, I find less and less to talk about with her."

"Everyone's the same." I tried to reassure him with his own words.

"True, but this goes beyond the norm. Daria's a very funny woman, pleasant and caring. She's a good mother, and she's very sexy." My heart shrank within me when he described Daria like that. "But she's a bit backward."

"What do you mean?"

"She doesn't grow up; she's not evolving… She's interested more or less in the same things that interested her when we were twenty. I sometimes feel frustrated, like we don't have too many things in common."

"It's the same with me," I blurted out without actually wanting to. He looked at me in astonishment.

"Really? You and David always looked to me like a perfect couple."

"Believe me, we're really, really far from perfect. I have a feeling, as well, that the passage of time has distanced us instead of bringing us closer."

"When I married Daria, I was sure that the fact that we were a little opposite would be the thing that would bring us closer. You know, they say opposites attract."

"It doesn't work that way," I said sadly.

"True."

We fell silent. I thought about my previous life, when we were married. We weren't a perfect couple .Now I knew that the perfect couple didn't exist, but our relationship was based on our similarities rather than our differences. We were interested in the same topics, loved to walk in the same places, we enjoyed the same movies and books, and we were good friends long before we were a romantic couple. With David, we were romantic partners first and then friends. And, unfortunately, like most couples, romance slowly faded away, and our friendship wasn't as strong as mine had been with Amir.

I sat and watched the Kineret. At first I was careful not to look at Amir. The confidences we had exchanged startled me, and I was scared to make eye contact with him. After a few minutes of staring, I didn't have to strain. The wind caressed my face, and a pleasant tranquility fell on all my limbs. I felt I was starting to fall asleep. I took a deep breath and turned to Amir. I was about to suggest we get back.

Amir's face told me everything. He was looking at me with the same look he had the first time he told me he loved me. I couldn't stop the tears from falling from my eyes,my and they broke free and washed my face. Amir leaned over and started kissing me passionately.

I wanted to stop him, but I couldn't... I couldn't. I missed him so much.

Within minutes, we were already joined to each other. Amir moaned with excitement. "How is that you know how to touch me like that?" he kept whispering.

The next day, I shut myself in our room. I didn't want to bump into Amir and, more than that, I didn't want to see Daria. I couldn't look her in the eye after I'd betrayed her like that. I told Inbal I wasn't feeling well and asked David if he wouldn't mind taking the girls to the activities she'd organized.

In the evening, we got together for Kabbalat Shabbat

in the kibbutz dining room. I sat and stared at my plate. I couldn't put a bite in my mouth. I focused on the plate... I was afraid to meet Amir's gaze.

"You're quite pale," Inbal said.

"True," Daria agreed. "If you're sick and you give whatever it is to my kids now, I'll kill you."

"I'm fine," I said weakly.

"You just don't look well," Inbal said anxiously. "Maybe you should go back to your room?" She looked at David and told him, "Walk her up to your room. I'll watch the girls in the meantime."

"It's okay," I said and got up. "I can go alone."

I left the dining room and started walking slowly back to our room. Tears streamed down my face. I felt my world was destroyed. I loved two men, one of whom I'd cheated on. I'd cheated on my friend. I'd ruined everyone's life.

Someone was running behind me. I turned around. It was Amir.

"What are you doing here?" I asked angrily. "Go to your wife!"

"I can't," he said, and tears began to spill from his eyes. "I can't say nothing passed between us yesterday... I can't continue as if nothing happened."

"But there's no choice!" I shouted in a whisper. "We're not going to destroy everybody's life because of one mistake."

"Mistake?" He looked at me, stunned. "Yesterday was a mistake?"

"Yes," I replied briefly.

"I'm in love with you... this can't be a mistake!" he said, and my heart almost burst out of my chest. "Until yesterday, I didn't believe it was mutual, that I had a chance, but now I know I do. You can't tell me you don't feel like I do. You couldn't touch me like that if the feeling weren't mutual."

"Amir," I said coldly. "Yesterday, we both got a bit carried away and had sex, and I'll tell you a secret. David cheated on me some time ago, and apparently I felt I needed to get back at him."

"I don't believe you," he said painfully.

"You'd better believe it," I said and went back to my room. I couldn't believe what I'd said, but if there was something I learned from the weird reality of my life, it was that the neighbor's grass is never really greener. It was nice to discover that, even in my new life, Amir desired me, but I didn't think it was worth breaking my family apart for. I'd already lived with Amir, and I knew the thrill would disappear.

CHAPTER 20

Once every few years, there's a bizarre story in the news of a woman giving birth without knowing she was pregnant. These stories have always entertained me. I could never understand how a woman couldn't know she was pregnant until the moment of the birth.

I was very close to being that woman.

In January 2012, I met Inbal in the mall by chance. At this stage of our lives, each of us had two children: Amir and Daria had Tom and Nofar (who were my children in my previous life), Asi and Inbal had Roy and Shira (Daria's children in my previous life) and David and I had two daughters, Coral and Adi(Inbal's daughters in our previous lives.) Because I knew that David had two daughters in his previous life, I wasn't expecting to be pregnant again in my present life. I expected Inbal, because she was with Asi, to declare her third pregnancy, because Asi was the only man who had three children in my previous life. Had I not discovered that Inbal wasn't pregnant, I, too, would have become one of those bizarre news items.

"I haven't seen or heard from you in ages," she scolded.

"Busy," I smiled sheepishly. I was really very busy at work, but mostly I was busy avoiding Daria.

"What are you doing?"

"Just shopping. I've been neglecting myself a little lately. I need to go on a diet. Lots of clothes don't fit me anymore!"

"Why diet if you can just do some shopping!" Inbal laughed.

"True," I laughed with her. I looked at her. She had a bit of a belly, and I assumed she was about four months pregnant. I was surprised she hadn't told me yet. "So you're pregnant?" I asked her tactlessly. I usually kept my mouth shut, but I was sure she was pregnant, not only because she had a bit of a belly, but because I knew she was due to give birth within six months.

"No." She looked at me, offended. "I've also put on a pound or two."

I was dumbfounded. She had to be pregnant. In the past four years, I'd predicted a hundred percent of all births in the group. She just had to be pregnant.

"Are you sure?" I asked her.

She looked at me, stunned. "Are you serious?" she asked. "Do you think I wouldn't know if I was pregnant?"

"Maybe you still don't want to tell me," I amazed myself with my insolence.

"Believe me, it's a little hard to be pregnant during your period." She told it like it was.

"Forgive me," I said sadly. "I probably really wanted you to be pregnant again."

"Me, too," she said sadly.

We said goodbye and my mind started working overtime. Inbal wasn't pregnant, but according to my calculations, Asi was supposed to father a third child in six months. Had Asi cheated on Inbal? Was another woman now expecting his third child? Maybe not all children from our previous life were going to be born in this one?

Maybe Asi wasn't Galia's biological father in our previous lives…

Once this thought occurred to me, all the symptoms of pregnancy broke out, my brain realized what had happened and within minutes, I was throwing up in the bathroom at the mall. Half an hour later, I was staring at the two lines of a positive pregnancy test.

I'd had sex with two men in my previous and present lives. I slept with both about three months ago too. After we'd gotten back from the weekend on the kibbutz, I'd made up with David and we'd experienced a new honeymoon phase. My conscience bothered me, but I also felt that my one-time stumble was payback for his one-time stumble.

If the fetus in my womb was Galia, Asi and Daria's third daughter in my previous life, then under the formula that determined the identity of the child by his father, that meant Daria cheated on Asi in my previous life. Was it with David? Or with Amir? Both had cheated in my new life. On the other hand, I wasn't sure I was carrying Galia in my womb. The simple formula that the father in the previous life was the father in this life no longer worked perfectly. I only knew with absolute certainty that Asi wasn't the father of my unborn child. He still could have been Galia's father in the previous life, because if I could cheat on David and David could cheat on me, and Amir, in our present life,

could cheat on Daria, then maybe Asi could have
cheated on Inbal and right now, little Galia was growing
in the womb of a woman I didn't even know!

David was beside himself with joy. Knowing he was
going to be a father for the third time overwhelmed him
with happiness. He was shocked that I discovered I was
pregnant at such an advanced stage, but was too happy
about it to really care. He hoped we'd finally have a
son. I hoped so too. It was the first time I didn't know
the sex of the baby before the ultrasound scan, and I
knew that a son meant I wasn't going to be Galia's
mother.

But it was a girl.

I had been pregnant four times - twice in my previous
life and twice in my present life. In none of the
pregnancies was I under such stress. Waiting for the
baby was nerve wracking. I could hardly concentrate on
work. I was a nervous wreck and, unfortunately, I
primarily took it out on David and the girls. They all
accepted my reaction with understanding because I was
pregnant. Everyone thought that the hormones were
making me mad, but I knew that what was driving me
crazy was the lack of knowledge. For the first time in my
present life, I didn't know to whom I was giving birth, or
who the father was. The strange reality of my life had
given me confidence over the years. Most of the time, I
knew what was going to happen, and for the first time in
my new life, I had to deal with an absolute lack of
knowledge.

My confusion grew when Daria told me that she was
pregnant too. In our previous lives, she was the only one
who got pregnant for a third time and now the both of
us were. She was expected to give birth in October 2012,
one month after my second accident. In my previous life,

when I was married to her husband, I wasn't pregnant for a third time. I was wondering if Amir was the father. Maybe Daria cheated on Amir?

Luckily, I didn't remember Galia's exact date of birth so I wasn't tense around a certain date. My estimated delivery date was the end of July, so I didn't change my work plans for the beginning of the month. On July 9th, I had a meeting with the tax assessor in Be'er Sheva. On the way, I was already feeling the contractions. I wasn't too concerned, because I always had some short contractions in my ninth month. During the meeting, a sharp pain pierced my body. More contractions came... it was clear I was in active labor. The assessment officer looked at me, panicked, and immediately asked his secretary to get me an ambulance urgently.

Between contractions, I updated my mother and David, who were both angry with me for driving to Be'er Sheva in this state. They couldn't get there in time for the birth. I was happy. I wanted to be alone. I wanted to meet my daughter without anyone who knew me watching. I didn't know what my reaction would be.

The birth was quick and easy, far more so than the four previous births, as if the baby was impatient to meet me too. I remembered how I'd had such trouble hugging Nofar immediately after she came out, but this time, I held out my arms expectantly, I so wanted to meet her.

Once they laid Galia in my arms, I had no doubt. I remembered the baby that I actually saw only once in my previous life, on the day of the second accident, from which I awoke in my new life. The memory of her sweet little face was etched in my memory. She looked at me quizzically, and I had a good feeling that she remembered me too. She was, and remained, the sweetest baby I've ever seen. I kissed her warmly and refused to part with her even for the nurse to clean her and perform the initial tests.

David arrived in the evening and found me nursing Galia. He looked at me with love in his eyes and came closer to get a good look at my child.

"Meet Galia," I smiled at him.

"Galia?" he asked.

"Yes, Galia," I replied. To me, she was born with that name.

"Nice name."

"Lovely name."

Galia nursed like no child had nursed from me in the past. From the first moment, the connection between us was just perfect, as if we'd known each other in another life. In fact, we had known each other in another life, only that time she had a different set of parents. I felt she came to the right mother this time.

David looked at me, hypnotized. He wasn't used to seeing me so warm and soft... so maternal. When Galia finished, I passed her to him. She cried - it was hard for her to part from me - but David quickly calmed her down with a loving embrace.

"She's amazing," he said.

I looked at the both of them. David was a wonderful father. He had an excellent way with children, but I didn't know if Galia was his daughter. Now that I knew Galia was my daughter, I realized that, in my previous life, Asi wasn't her father. Daria had an affair with either David or Amir. One of them was Galia's father now - and one of the two was her father in my previous life. If Galia was David's daughter, then, in spite of his many promises that he could never cheat on me 'all the way,' it seemed he was able to do so when he was married to Inbal. And if Galia was Amir's daughter, then I was cheated on as his wife in my previous life. It was sixteen years since I'd lived my life with Amir, and I'd forgotten most of the negative memories over time, but now I remembered how impatient I was with Amir. I remembered being a sad and bitter woman. The thought that Amir's betrayal - if Galia was his daughter - was justified, hadn't even crossed my mind and I figured that if I'd discovered the betrayal in my previous life, I would have found it very difficult to understand and forgive him. Now that a lot of time had passed and I had made dramatic changes in my present life, I had to admit that I wasn't an easy or supportive spouse to Amir, and I should shoulder my fair share of blame in making Amir distance himself from me.

What was it about me that made men cheat on me? Or rather, what was wrong with me? I had no doubt that the two men in my life loved me very much, but something made them drift away from me to the point of cheating. In my previous life, I was a bitter and sad woman, so I'd made sure that everything in my present, professional life wouldn't make me bitter again, which led me to distance myself physically and psychologically from my spouse.

I decided to learn the lesson that Galia's birth taught me. When Galia was a month old, I went to the office. Some of the girls from the office clustered around the stroller and fawned over my sweet baby. I couldn't miss the astonished looks I got from some of the other women, lawyers, who were shocked by the maternal surge that I suddenly enjoyed. For most lawyers, two children was a kind of necessity, in order to establish a 'normal' family, but a third child was an unwanted hindrance to their career.

I went to see Jacob, the senior partner, with Galia in

my arms. He smiled the fake smile I knew he mostly reserved for clients. "Congratulations," he said. "She's a cute little thing. How old is she now?" He tried to fake some interest.

"Five-and-a-half weeks," I replied and got straight to the matter that had brought me here. I knew that his interest in me and my daughter was non-existent, and I wanted to finish what I had to say, "I wanted to let you know that, this time, unlike with my previous children, I'm going to extend my maternity leave."

I knew he didn't like my announcement, but he was also a lawyer and knew that, legally, he couldn't say one single word about it or threaten my livelihood. He continued to smile his fake smile, and when I explained my plans, he wished me luck and added that he'd be awaiting my return at the end of my maternity leave. He had no choice.

Maternity 'leave' is a misleading name for the first few months of a baby's life, when his mother stays at home to care for him. Even though the mother doesn't work, calling this period of time 'leave,' as though the mother's on vacation, is stretching it a bit. My previous maternity 'leaves' were very difficult for me. I didn't feel free from work at all, but this time, with Galia, I did enjoy a sense of freedom. I was much more relaxed and comfortable. Galia was also a much more manageable baby than my other children. She allowed my hidden maternal instinct to blossom. David looked at me in wonder and love. He'd waited years to see me like this. His gaze tormented me, however, because I still didn't know if he was Galia's father or not.

Galia had been my daughter for almost two months now, but Daria and Inbal had not met her yet. They asked repeatedly to meet up, but I rejected their requests. I knew that a group meeting would put Amir in the same room with his possible daughter. Almost a year had passed since that fateful trip to the kibbutz, and Amir and I hadn't met even once since. Eventually, I had to invite the group to meet my Galia. Inbal, Asi and their children arrived first, and I waited restlessly for Daria and Amir's arrival. David didn't understand why I was so tense about this friendly get-together. Obviously, I couldn't explain myself to him.

Daria arrived, only with Nofar. She claimed Tom was sick and Amir had volunteered to stay home with him. Almost sixteen years ago, I used that exact same excuse when I went to the party Daria organized in honor of Galia's birth. Tom really was a bit sick, but Amir really did insist on staying home with him.

I knew I had to solve the mystery of Galia's father's identity. I didn't know if it would change anything, but not knowing, a feeling that was so unfamiliar to me in my present life, was just not an option. While all the children were in the playroom, I snuck up behind Nofar and cut a small strand of her hair. The next day, I sent it to a lab with hair that I cut from David's head while he slept and with a saliva sample I took from Galia's mouth.

I waited seventeen nerve-wracking days for the answer. I got it exactly on my thirty-second birthday, sixteen years after my second accident, my birthday present.

Galia wasn't David's biological daughter. She was Nofar's sister.

EPILOGUE

Yesterday was my forty-eighth birthday.

I'm forty-eight years old now, but in my mind, I'm sixty-four. I woke up at the age of sixteen, but I was actually thirty-two.

On my thirty-second birthday, when I discovered that Galia was Amir's daughter, I waited in terror for the end of the day. I was afraid that once again, I'd be involved in an accident and wake up sixteen again. I didn't want to get stuck in an endless cycle... I've had enough lifetimes. Thankfully, a day later, I lived to be thirty-two and a day, just as, today, I'm forty-eight and a day old.

I was afraid to go back in time again. My new life wasn't perfect, but the fact that I relived the sixteen years after my first car accident taught me that there's no such thing as a perfect life.

My pregnancy with Galia prepared me for my life after I turned thirty-two. After sixteen years in which I had almost no surprises in my life, from the age of thirty-two, every moment of my life was new and unknown. It took me some time to get used to a reality in which I didn't have an advantage over the rest of mankind, a reality in which my secret super power had expired. It was a reality that brought me tremendous relief because I didn't need to pretend anymore.

Once I got used to my new reality, I learned to enjoy life more than I ever had before in my old and new thirty-two years put together. I learned that there was no point in trying to always be in control. I realized that, no matter how much I planned, each person had his own destiny. I still believe that every person is the master of his fate, but I know that some things can't be stopped. I couldn't stop Galia from coming into this world.

Inbal and Asi had twins. Asi's business almost went bankrupt, but Inbal stood beside him with love and dedication. Their love triumphed over their difficulties, and Asi has begun to make a success of himself again, even more so than before. I'm happy for Inbal, and realize that, by choosing David in my new life, I led her into Asi's arms, and I often have the feeling that this alone was a good enough reason for everything I went through.

Daria and Amir got divorced. Daria's baby, born a month after my thirty-second birthday, wasn't Amir's, and he found out about it. I often wondered who the father was. I didn't ask and she didn't tell. However, I couldn't ignore the fact that Aya, Lior's wife, hadn't gotten pregnant for a third time in our present lives.

David and I have stayed together. We have our ups and downs, some of them still have to do with my stressful job, which I refuse to give up despite the fact that he disapproves, but I know David is my soul mate, my destiny. I've never told him - and am not planning on telling him - that Galia is not his daughter. If there was one more conclusion that my special life has taught me, it's that being a biological parent means nothing. Parenthood doesn't come from birth. It's created from years of love, nurture and education given to the child. David loves Galia dearly, and she loves him. She is his daughter just as she is mine.

DEAR READER

I hope you had a pleasant reading experience. If you enjoyed the book, I'd be very grateful if you'd take another minute of your time and leave a positive review for the book on its Amazon page. If you liked *Déjà Vu*, I think you'll find *Confession of An Abandoned Wife* interesting as well.

Déjà vu is my third book – written after I swore that I wouldn't write any more books. My first two, *Confession of An Abandoned Wife* and *Hill of Secrets* were published in Israel in Hebrew in early 2011 and 2013 respectively. Both books received enthusiastic reviews among professional reviewers. *Confession of An Abandoned Wife* was almost published through one of the largest and most well-thought-out publishing campaigns in Israel. But it didn't happen, and I financed the book's publication through small expenditures. I believed in myself and my books, mainly because non-related professionals believed in them. I thought the books would become best-sellers, but it didn't happen – not because the books are no good, or uninteresting, but because of the Israeli book market. In Israel, the digital book market hardly exists. It's started to change in the last few years, but it's still very far from the situation in other places. The handful of Israeli readers prefer to read books in printed format. It's important to note that, in Israel, there's a whole sector of the population who can't use a digital reader for religious reasons on Saturdays and holidays – and these are the days when most people like to read! Because the printed format is almost exclusive in Israel, the market supply is huge, and the price of each printed book is low. In order for the writer and publisher to make a marginal profit from the sale of each copy, they must pre-print large quantities in order to keep printing costs down. What actually happens for most writers is that they get stuck with a large inventory of books and a bottom line loss.

In June 2013, a few months after my second book, *Hill of Secrets*, was published, I participated in the Book Week Market in Rabin Square, the main square in Tel Aviv. I didn't sell a single book to the best of my memory, and I wasn't the only one. There were very few buyers, and a rather sad atmosphere. I realized that, although I had ideas for at least ten books, I had no audience, so there was no point in continuing to write. It was depressing, but also liberating.

At that time, I began to receive ads for an online course for selling books on Amazon. At first, I ignored it, but later, I became intrigued. The economist in me suddenly realized that the problem was not in me, but in the market, and if I wanted to sell my books, I simply need to change my market! In July 2014, I published *Hill of Secrets* on Amazon and was amazed to find that my book sold to English speakers who know very little about life in Israel. Later, I also published my first book, *Confession of An Abandoned Wife*. In October 2014, Liron Fine, the guy who taught me how to sell books on Amazon.com, interested me in the Israeli Nanowrimo competition. For those who don't know the rules of competition, this is a competition in which the participants must write a book during the month of November. At the end of the month, they have to submit a draft. Almost a year-and-a-half after swearing that I'd never write any more books, I decided to return to the keyboard. My short experience with Amazon proved to me that I had an audience to write for after all. I guess there are quite a few writers who come to this competition with ready handwriting, but I hadn't written anything for about two years! I had nothing on paper, but my mind was bursting with ideas. I wanted to write about a topic that preoccupies me a lot. What would happen if...

I knew most of the plot of *Déjà Vu* in advance. I wanted to examine the lives of three female friends in two situations in life. Although I'm not a big fan of science fiction, I decided to present the story in a way that has no logical explanation. I don't think it damages the story. I actually ended up with a combination of *Sliding Doors* and *Groundhog Day*. In order to give a twist to the story, I threw in an added issue – that of the true parentage of one of the children, and the subsequent discovery of a betrayal! But, beyond this aspect, the main idea of the book is our decision-making process as human beings and the obvious conclusion that each person should be complete within himself. I have certainly made – and will make again – quite a few mistakes in my life, but I try not to say that I regret my choices. My choices have led me to where I am today, and I'm at peace with myself.

Although there's a supernatural element in the book, this is the book in which I've included the most elements of my personal life, as if I were examining myself personally. I invite you to visit my Facebook page

(Michal Hartstein - Israeli writer) to receive updates on new posts, book deals, and, of course, keep up with new books to be published.

I hope I've intrigued you enough to read more of my books!

Yours,
Michal

ABOUT THE AUTHOR

Michal Hartstein was born in 1974 in Israel into a religious family, studied economics and accounting at the University of Tel Aviv and started a career in finance.

In 2006, after becoming a mother, she decided to change direction and began to write. For several years, she has written a popular personal blog, and in 2011 published her first book, *Confession of an Abandoned Wife*. After two years she published her second book, *Hill of Secrets*. In 2014 she participated in the Israeli Nanowrimo contest and wrote *Déjà Vu*. The book was one of the winners and was published in Israel in 2015. Her fourth book, *The Hit*, (the second book in the Hadas Levinger series) was published in 2018.

Ms. Hartstein's books vividly describe the life of the Israeli middle class, focusing on middle class women.

Made in the USA
Columbia, SC
17 March 2021